4284

..s, Charlie,

...ent down
...a

THE DEVIL WENT DOWN TO GEORGIA

STORIES BY CHARLIE DANIELS

PEACHTREE PUBLISHERS, LTD.

4284

Published by
PEACHTREE PUBLISHERS, LTD.
494 Armour Circle, N.E.
Atlanta, Georgia 30324

Manufactured in the United States of America

2nd printing

Library of Congress Catalog Number 85-62665

ISBN 0-931948-85-1

Dedicated with love to my mother and dad,
LaRue and Carlton Daniels.

There just ain't nobody like Mama and Daddy.

Contents

THE DEVIL WENT DOWN TO GEORGIA

The Story
Behind the Stories

WHEN MY PUBLISHER told me he would like to have a brief autobiography to go along with my short stories, I was a little hesitant. That story has a beginning, I told him, but I'm still working on the middle and the end. So he said he'd settle for the beginning, which is exactly where I'm gonna start.

To look at me today, some people might have a hard time believing I was ever a little fellow, but the truth is that I used to weigh only seven pounds and twelve ounces. That was back on October 28, 1936, when I was born at the James Walker Memorial Hospital in Wilmington, North Carolina. The birth of a son to William Carlton Daniels and LaRue Hammonds Daniels was an inauspicious occasion, with the possible exception that I was the first grandchild born on my mother's side of the family. They named me Charles Edwards and took me home, as bald-headed as a billiard ball and destined to be an only child.

It was a different world I entered that early fall morning,

for I was born into an isolated Jim Crow South where life was simple and change came slowly. The worst of the Great Depression was behind us and the Big War was still ahead. Franklin Delano Roosevelt was president, Cokes cost a nickel, everybody drove used cars (if they drove at all), and almost everybody went to church at least once in a while.

My home state of North Carolina was first-growth, long-leaf pine trees and pristine dirt roads with broad rivers and narrow bridges. Few people there went to college, and New York City seemed as far away as the moon.

Wilmington was a picturesque old city of about forty thousand people, a seaport town with pink and white azalea bushes and massive old live oak trees with Spanish moss hanging from their branches. The Cape Fear River meandered through downtown, and the Atlantic Ocean was about ten miles away.

The old house we lived in is on the outskirts of Wilmington today, but in the late thirties and early forties it was considered quite a ways out of the city. And by today's standards, that old house was quite primitive. It had electricity but no indoor plumbing. We had a hand pump on the back porch and an outhouse in the back yard. And yes, friends, it's true — the Sears and Roebuck catalog spent its last days in the outhouse, growing smaller by the day. The first erotic pictures I ever saw were the ladies modeling lingerie on the pages of that famous catalog.

All of our heat in the winter came from a wood-burning stove. I remember taking baths in a galvanized washtub with the side of me toward the fire burning up and the other side freezing.

Other early memories are a little less vivid. I remember

riding a green tricycle on the front porch, because that was the only place I had to ride. There weren't any sidewalks out where we lived. And I remember a little black puppy my daddy brought home in his coat one day. I also remember the hurt when that little dog was run over.

I'm sure that time has colored my memories to some extent, but it seemed that when we lived on the Carolina Beach Road that the moon would shine brighter than it ever has since. And there were so many stars that the night sky looked like country butter stirred up in grandma's molasses.

At a pretty young age, I discovered family in general and grandparents in particular. My daddy, Carlton, came from a big, close-knit family of three boys and six girls. There was Johnnie, Jewel, Mabel, Odell, Ila, Ona, Egbert and Marvin.

Although my paternal grandfather passed away very early in my life, my grandmother, Grandma Daisy, was full of life and I loved her with all my heart. She was a pious woman with long chestnut hair that she wore up in a bun behind her head. She was fat and jolly and the very epitome of what a grandma's supposed to be.

Grandma Daisy lived on a farm about two and a half miles out the Peanut Road from Elizabethtown, in Bladen County, about fifty-five miles from Wilmington.

A visit to her house was a real treat. It meant riding the mules and playing with my cousins Murray and Hector Van and Walton and Jimmy and Mack and Clayton, not to mention our friend, Pete Perkins. There was a creek with a swimming hole and nearby a grove of pecan trees where we went with Grandma Daisy to gather pecans.

Charlie Daniels

Her old homeplace was even more primitive than our house. It had no electricity and no running water, but Grandma Daisy cooked scrumptious Southern meals on a wood cookstove, and the water from the well was clear and sweet. There was always homemade butter and fresh watermelon in the summertime, and fireplaces and flatirons and kerosene lamps and fluffy feather beds that sank down in the middle when you lay down on them — all sorts of things to charm a boy my age.

Most of my daddy's brothers and sisters lived within a few miles of the old homeplace, and we saw a lot of them during our visits. On Sunday afternoons a multitude of neighbors and kinfolks would gather up at Grandma's house. The ladies would sit around the front room and talk about somebody's thyroid condition, while the men would stand around in the yard discussing the finer points of bluetick hound dogs and the price of fertilizer.

Invariably someone would sit down at Grandma Daisy's old, out of tune, upright piano, and the first thing you knew the front room was full of people singing.

They sang old hymns mostly, and once in a while some old obscure songs that I've never heard anyplace else.

"Mildred, play 'Power In The Blood.' "

"Yeah, and then let's do 'Leave Them Browns Alone.' "

And so it went with "The Old Rugged Cross" and "Amazing Grace," "Just A Little Talk With Jesus" and "When The Roll Is Called Up Yonder."

And then Mrs. Mollie Singletary would sit down to the piano and play my favorite. It was called "And The Whale Did," and Mrs. Mollie would be sitting there banging away on that old upright piano for all she was worth with a

4

That's me, before glasses, at about age five.

Overalls were part of my fifth grade attire. Below, that's me at my granddaddy's house in Wilmington. Nice legs, huh?

Cousin Merle and I visit Grandmother's house.

Charlie Daniels

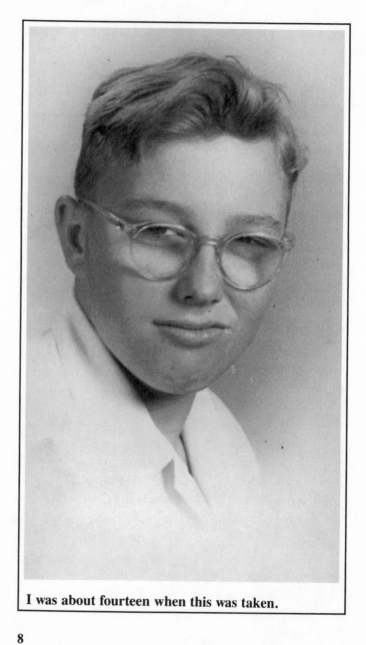

I was about fourteen when this was taken.

room full of people singing:

> "And the whale did
> And the whale did
> Yes the whale did
> Swallow Jonah down."

Oh, I just loved it. I do believe that was the only song Mrs. Mollie Singletary knew how to play, but it was enough.

And finally somebody would say, "Gladys, I reckon we better go." And then would begin a Southern ritual that was repeated every time good people would get together.

"Oh, y'all don't need to go. Stay around and have something to eat with us."

"Naw, I guess we better go. I've got to milk the cow before we go to church. Y'all come go with us."

"Naw, I reckon we better stay around here. But I wish y'all wouldn't leave."

"Well, we appreciate it, but we better run on. Y'all come see us. Marvin, I'll be on over here early in the morning."

And early it was, for it was a sunup till sundown proposition when you raised bright leaf tobacco for a living.

You had to plant the seeds in a bed and cover them with netting, in hopes that the frost didn't kill the young plants. Then you pulled the healthiest plants in the spring and transplanted them in the field, hoping that they would take hold and grow. Then you fertilized it, ploughed it, suckered it, hoed it, sprayed it for worms and hoped that you'd make a crop.

About twelve weeks later you harvested it by picking one leaf at a time, strung it on sticks, hung the sticks in the barn, cured it, took the sticks out of the barn, took the tobacco off the sticks, graded it, tied it and hauled it to market, hoping that you made enough money to pay off the debts you'd incurred during the year being a tobacco farmer.

In other words, I guess you could say that raising tobacco was ninty-nine percent hard work and ninety-nine percent hope, and if that adds up to 198 percent, so be it. That's how it was.

The men in my father's family had weather-worn faces and calloused hands. They were farmers and sawmill men, and they worked in the log woods.

You couldn't say that they were educated men, though they were all literate. On the average, they may have completed the eighth grade or so. But they had a healthy respect for education. My cousin Walton was the first male child on the Daniels side of the family to finish high school. It was such a big occasion that we drove into Elizabethtown from about eighty miles away to see him graduate.

But mostly the Daniels men just put in day after day of hard, honest work and raised their families the best way they knew how.

Everybody used to go to town on Saturday, so the streets of Elizabethtown would be crawling with people. There'd be little knots of people standing on the street talking — men in bib overalls and khaki pants and ladies in clean print dresses.

There'd also be barefooted little boys, hurrying off down the street to the Bladen Theater to sit through three cartoons, two cowboy movies and a chapter of whatever black-and-white serial that happened to be running.

Nobody appreciates Saturday like a country boy. It was a magical day, filled with popcorn and chocolate ice cream sodas and Roy Rogers and Gene Autry and Bob Steele. It was the most successful social happening I've ever attended.

Oh, once in a while somebody would show up in town as drunk as a bicycle (much to the disgust of the good local ladies).

"Did you see him, Viola? He was so drunk he couldn't hardly stand up. I said to Blanche, I said, 'Blanche, look at him staggering around over yonder. He ought to be ashamed of hisself. His mama would just die if she seen him.' "

Bladen was a dry county at the time, as were most of the rural counties in the state, which suited the bootleggers just fine.

Then when Saturday afternoon turned to Saturday night, it was off for home to a standard supper of hotdogs and Pepsi-Colas and the Grand Ole Opry.

I can't begin to tell you what an impact the Grand Ole Opry had on the rural southeast.

650-WSM came booming down our way all the way from Nashville, Tennessee, sounding for all the world like a local station, and everybody listened to the Grand Ole Opry. Roy Acuff owned Saturday night. He was the King as I know of no other man being in my lifetime. He still is in my book.

Sunday morning at Grandma's meant Sunday school and church at Wesley's Chapel. My daddy's side of the family were all Methodists with nary a Baptist in the bunch, which is pretty unusual in the Deep South. They all believed in God and passed that faith on to me at an

11

Charlie Daniels

early age.

In fact, I've never been able to understand why some people have so much trouble believing in God. It only takes a look around at the intricacies of life to realize that there is definitely a higher power.

My beliefs are pretty simple. I believe that God has always been and always will be. I believe that He is all powerful and that He created the universe and everything in it.

I believe that Jesus Christ is the only begotten Son of God, born of a Virgin. I believe that He died on a cross to atone for our sins, and that on the third day He arose from the dead and ascended into Heaven. And I believe that He will return to earth someday.

That's pretty much the philosophy my daddy was raised with, and it worked all right for him. He was an honest, self-reliant man who loved music and singing, joking and laughing, good people and good food and his work.

He knew more about pine timber than any man I ever knew. He could look at a tree and tell you within a fraction how many board feet of lumber it would make after it was cut down.

He was gentle and caring and he loved very deeply. Especially my mama.

Daddy told me that the first time he ever saw my mama she was wearing a pair of cut-off overalls, and he thought she was the prettiest thing he'd ever seen. She certainly was a strikingly pretty woman in her youth. The boys I played with were always telling me how pretty my mama was. She was only seventeen when she married Daddy.

My mother would tackle anything. I remember her

12

Happiness is a shotgun and a mandolin . . .

. . . and a couple of Granddaddy's hunting dogs.

In 1955, some buddies and I
took our first trip to the Grand
Ole Opry. Below, (l-r) that's
Ted Phillips, Lawson Barber,
me, Jimmy Phillips and Russell
Palmer. On the next page,
that's me strutting in the hotel
and us stopping at a diner on
the way home.

At a live radio broadcast, that's Bill Pollard (l),
Dean Wall (c) and me sawing on the fiddle.

working on our old Zenith radio with a kitchen knife. She didn't know anything at all about working on radios, but somehow, miraculously, she always made it work.

She came from a smaller family than Daddy's, but just as close-knit. In addition to her, there was Ruby, Greta and John, who we called Buster.

Just like my daddy, my mama came from a line of good, hard-working folks. My maternal great-great-grandfather came to this country from Ireland. He worked on a riverboat that ran up and down the Cape Fear River and was killed when a boiler blew up. Till this day his family doesn't know the exact spot where he was buried.

My granddaddy's name was Charles Graham Hammonds. He was a tremendously strong man, physically and in his heart and soul. When he was a young man, he carried a bale of cotton (which weighs about five hundred pounds) on his back all the way around a small barn. Just to see if he could do it. Or maybe to win a bet.

Granddaddy was a master hunter and fisherman, could build a boat or a house and always had the most beautiful vegetable garden you ever laid eyes on. He was resourceful and compassionate and was loved and respected as much as any man I ever knew.

My grandmother was Mattie Lee Suggs, before she married Granddaddy, and if God ever made a sweeter woman, I've never met her. She was the gentlest person I've ever known, and one of her biggest pleasures in life was cooking huge Southern-style meals and watching people enjoy eating them.

Needless to say, I always gave a good amount of myself when I put my feet under my grandmother's table. We'd have a big platter of fried chicken, rice and gravy, speckled butter beans and cream-style Silver Queen corn, collard greens, big old biscuits and iced tea that'd already been sweetened. Now, you can't sit down to a spread like that and ask somebody to pass the cottage cheese.

In the spring of the year, Granddaddy would string a net across Town Creek and catch herring plump with roe. We'd fry them up on the creek bank and eat them with hush puppies and cole slaw. Next morning we'd have fresh herring roe fried with eggs. Good eating just ran in the family.

Mattie and Graham, as their friends called my grandparents, were married for almost sixty-seven years and had a profound influence on my life. They lived just down the road from us and I used to spend a lot of time with them.

I particularly liked being there when Aunt Ethel came to spend the night. She told the best ghost stories I've ever heard. I think my favorite was the one about the empty rocking chair that would rock when they turned the lights off. I would sit there and listen and almost be afraid to go to bed. Aunt Ethel's stories were all supposedly true.

I was at my grandparents' house that cold, gray Sunday in December when the bombs fell on Pearl Harbor. I was only five at the time, but I remember it was a grim day.

Shortly after the war started, Daddy went to work for the Atlantic Coastline Railroad, and they shipped us off to Valdosta, Georgia. Housing was hard to come by during the war, so we lived in the Daniel Ashley Hotel for several weeks. I'd never been very far away from Wilmington, and the most lonesome sight I've ever seen was looking out the windows of that hotel down onto the unfamiliar streets of Valdosta.

It was a traumatic experience for a six-year-old country boy who was used to running barefoot through the Bermuda grass of coastal North Carolina to be suddenly cooped up on the fifth floor of a hotel.

In the meantime, I started school and made some new friends. I think I would have liked Valdosta, but I just wasn't around long enough to find out. Between the time I finished the first grade and started the third, we chased the creosote industry back to Wilmington, then to Elizabethtown, to Wilmington again and finally to Baxley, Georgia.

Baxley was one of those sleepy little south Georgia towns with a clock tower on the courthouse and one movie theater. I had my first real job in Baxley one summer. I was a water boy in a tobacco warehouse, and if my memory serves me correctly, it paid twelve and a half dollars a week.

By the time I started fifth grade, we had moved to Goldston, North Carolina. The school was called Goldston High School, but it could have been called Goldston Elementary, Junior High and High School, because it was all of that. All together, there were three hundred and some students in twelve grades.

We lived about ten miles out of Goldston in Chatham County in a big old farmhouse that came complete with a milk cow and a collie dog. There was a creek at the foot of the property where I'd catch little perch, and Mama would fry them up for me. On Saturday night, my friends Charles and Horton Seagroves and Clarence Johnson would come over to our house and we'd roast weenies out in the yard.

I got my first shotgun for Christmas that year — an Iver Johnson twenty-gauge single barrel. That qualified me as a real hunter, and all the men in my family liked to hunt.

I remember a year when Daddy went coon hunting every night during the month of October. It was against the law to hunt on Sunday, so he'd get up at midnight, which made it Monday morning, and go. I used to go with him pretty often. I loved hearing the dogs run and listening to the men around the fire telling stories of past hunts and things they used to do when they were boys. I suspect most of it was probably pretty well inflated, but it sure made interesting listening.

The next summer I worked in the woods with Daddy and met a lot of people I guess I'll remember the rest of my life. There was Dewitt and Peewee and Agie and Merk and O.C. and Johnny, all gentlemen with stories to tell just like the hunting crowd. Maybe that's when my appreciation for good storytelling began.

I got through the fifth grade and part of the sixth before we left Goldston. I eventually graduated from Goldston High School, but not before attending school again in Wilmington; Elizabethtown; Spartanburg, South Carolina; and Wilmington one more time.

I can't say that I regret all that moving around we did when I was a kid, cause it was an education in itself. But it got kind of aggravating. I'd have a set of friends in one town and then next thing you knew we were in a new town with a whole new set of friends to make and a whole new set of bullies to face.

I've always been big for my age, and when I'd walk into a new classroom, some knothead would feel that his "baddest boy in the class" status was being threatened and he'd proceed to take me on.

My daddy told me early on not to start a fight, but

Before hitting the road: (l-r) Joe Phillips, me, my dad and Russell Palmer.

I did vocals for our band called the Rockets.

I've always spent a lot of time practicing.

The Rockets playing North Beach, Maryland, 1958.

Charlie Daniels

Norman Tyson (l) backs up my vocals.

24

he said, "Charles, if you've got to fight, don't pay no attention to how much he's hurting you. Just keep on hurting him."

Well, thanks to Daddy's advice and a whole lot of unwanted experience, I guess I did all right.

The last time we moved back to Chatham County, we didn't live in the country. No sir, we lived smack in the middle of downtown Gulf, North Carolina.

Gulf, or *the* Gulf as some folks called it, was a wide place in the road, State Route 421 to be exact. It had three filling stations, one general store and a Presbyterian church. Gulf was no metropolis by any stretch of the imagination, but let me tell you something, friend, the Gulf was happening in the early fifties. We might have been a one-horse town, but we rode that old horse to death.

A lot happened to me while I was living in Gulf. I started smoking cigarettes and tasted my first beer. The cigarettes I stole from my daddy, until he caught me, and the beer we pilfered from the Budweiser warehouse. It was hotter than the cigarettes.

I also had my first real date, held down my first steady job, and almost ended my hopes of being a musician by cutting off the first knuckle of my right ring finger with a ripsaw. We were building a set for the senior play, and I got a little careless. The first thing I thought of when I looked down — it hadn't even started bleeding yet — was thank goodness it was on my right hand instead of my left. It would be tough making chords with a short finger, but I can pick just fine with it.

I also saw television for the first time in Gulf. It was at Russell Palmer's house, since his family had one of the first television sets in the area. People used to show up in droves to watch it, no matter what was on the one station they received.

Me and Tommy Wilkie practically lived at Russell's house. And then some nights our friends Ralph and Ernest Willets and Joe Phillips and Jimmy Phillips and no telling who else would show up. Russell lived with his daddy and an uncle and aunt, and I'll never know how they put up with us. Can you imagine going home intending to spend the evening watching television only to find your living room full of teen-age boys who keep talking and slipping outside to smoke cigarettes?

It was a good old bunch of boys who lived in the Gulf in those days, and we really had a good time. We were never really mean, but we were always into some kind of mischief.

I remember the time that we made a dummy, stuck a knife in his chest and laid him at the railroad crossing. He really looked like a dead man. We hid down by the railroad and waited for someone to come by.

The first one to come along was Alvy Millikin. When he saw the dummy, he jerked his car in reverse and went tearing off down to Herbert Palmer's house. Herbert was Russell's daddy and a deputy sheriff. Alvy went flying up in the yard and told them that he had to see Herbert, that there was a man laying dead up at the railroad crossing.

Herbert wasn't home but Russell was, and he informed Alvy that it was just a dummy some of us boys had made. Whereupon Alvy made a statement to the effect of, "If every damn body in the Gulf was laying dead side of the road, I wouldn't stop no more," and went home.

One day when I was sitting around at Russell Palmer's

house, he casually pulled out a Stella guitar and proceeded to play about two and a half chords. Well, I immediately went crazy. I had had a secret desire to play a guitar almost all my life, or at least since those childhood days of listening to the Grand Ole Opry. But I'd never had anybody to learn from. Now here was my best buddy with a guitar that he knew almost three chords on.

Nothing would do but he just had to show me how. I got to where I could play a G chord pretty quick, but from there on it was pretty tough slogging. Anyway, I kept on trying and after a while I could play G pretty damn good, and I could even hit C and D once in a while.

I decided that it was time for me to make my debut. My first dressing room was a pantry, my first stage was the kitchen floor and my first audience was my parents.

Mama and Daddy had gone somewhere, and when I heard them coming back in the house, I hid in the pantry with Russell's Stella guitar. When they walked into the kitchen, I jumped out playing G (and sometimes C and D) for all I was worth. My parents got a real kick out of it, never dreaming of the dark days to come when they would have to listen to me learning how to play.

I did an awful lot of practicing in those days. I never had what you'd call natural talent as a musician, so I had to practice hard on every instrument I ever learned to play. And if I ever found anyone around town who could play, I'd bug them until they taught me what they knew.

I really wanted to learn how to play that guitar. But just about the time I got to where I could play C and D with some semblance of regularity, Tommy Wilkie showed up one day with a mandolin.

It was too much for me. I just had to get my hands on

that mandolin, and then it was more months of ear-grind-ing practice before I could do much more than look at it.

Russell and I practiced together all the time, and he was really coming along on the guitar. Then he got a new guitar, a Gibson, the first really good instrument that any of us ever had ahold of. It was head and shoulders above the old Stella that we'd all started with.

Here, I'd like to take the opportunity to say something to parents whose children want to learn to play. Buy them a good instrument. Bad instruments are hard to learn on and they make your fingers so sore that you may very well give up on it before you really give it a chance.

Somewhere along about that time, Joe Phillips got ahold of a five-string banjo and started showing up to practice with us once in a while. We started learning whole songs, and since I'd always loved to sing, I started learning the lyrics.

One night we got to talking and decided that it was time for the world to hear us. Hell, we knew five or six songs. What we needed was a public appearance. Someplace where the public could come and hear this new phe-nomenon that was springing forth out of the Gulf.

Somehow we got the idea of doing our maiden concert as a benefit for a needy local gentleman. That very same night we went out and got some cardboard and made posters announcing the debut of "The Misty Mountain Boys" at the Gulf Community Building on a Saturday night in the not-too-distant future.

We didn't ask anyone's permission to use the commu-nity building or anything else, we just did it.

Now, don't go getting any delusions of grandeur when I talk about the Gulf Community Building. It was an old

At home with good friends and a good cigar, 1960.

That's me and a hairy friend at the Shreveport Fair, 1966.

brick building with one room about forty by twenty-five.

Our next problem was coming up with a public address system. The only person in our neck of the woods who had anything remotely resembling a public address system was Poochie Reeves, who had a National guitar amplifier that his daddy had got drunk and bought one day for some unknown reason. We went down to the Reeves residence and borrowed Poochie's amplifier. We also borrowed a microphone from somebody or other and we were in business.

The big night finally arrived and we must have had about twenty people, counting our mamas and daddies.

The stage was set (the stage was some boards laid across two sawhorses), the audience was in their seats and the red light on Poochie Reeves's amplifier was glowing like a beacon. And then we took the stage — Russell Palmer on guitar, Joe Phillips on five-string banjo and Charlie Daniels on mandolin and vocals, as well as handling the master of ceremonies chores.

We played our extremely limited repertoire, which the audience seemed to enjoy. But it was a short show, to say the least. The big hit of the night was Ralph Willets, who sang an off-key version of "I'm Gonna Kill Myself" while accompanying himself on the guitar, which he didn't know one damn chord on. His unscheduled appearance broke the place up.

But we had done it. We had raised a few dollars for a worthy cause and thought sure that we were off and running, with fame and fortune just around the corner. After we learned about three more songs, we decided that we needed us a radio program.

There were a lot of local bands playing on the small

31

town stations in those days. It paid absolutely nothing and gave the radio station a lot of free programming, so they were receptive to the idea.

I think it was Russell Palmer who finally worked up enough nerve to call radio station WWGP in Sanford and set up an audition. We considered ourselves to be a bluegrass band, and our name, "The Misty Mountain Boys," was a direct rip-off from "Lester Flatt, Earl Scruggs and The Foggy Mountain Boys," who were our idols.

We practiced hard and when the fateful day arrived, we started for Sanford with the good wishes of our families and friends and phrases like, "Y'all are as good as some of 'em I hear on the radio," ringing in our ears.

We knew we were in trouble, however, when we saw Harry Barfield, the station manager. He was a businesslike, no-nonsense sort of a man who listened to our music, offered some valid criticism, and then burst our bubble. We headed back to the Gulf in disgrace to face our family and friends and tell them that there would be no radio show forthcoming for The Misty Mountain Boys.

We were kind of down in the mouth about not getting the radio show, but youth has its advantages, one being the ability to forever bounce back. So before long we were practicing hard again.

Just about the time I started to figure out the mandolin a little bit, somebody showed up with a fiddle and I was gone again. Back to the day-in, day-out practicing, squeaking and squawking. It's a wonder my parents didn't move away and leave me while I was at school. Pat Thomas once said that when I played the fiddle, it sounded like somebody had stepped on a cat. I guess it did.

The first money I ever made playing it was one Saturday

night when Russell and me were sitting around the filling station with the fiddle and guitar, hoping somebody would ask us to play a tune. A car pulled up and two men and two pretty girls got out. I think they'd all been drinking pretty heavy, and one of the ladies, upon seeing the instruments, asked us if we'd play something.

Well, Russell Palmer piped right up and said, "Have you got any money?" The lady reached in her purse and pulled out four dimes, twenty cents apiece. And we proceeded to play. I really enjoyed making that twenty cents.

Meanwhile, I was still trying to finish high school. Goldston was a small school by almost anybody's standards; the class of '55 was only twenty-two strong.

I'm sure that we didn't have some of the advantages that bigger schools have, but we also had advantages that bigger schools could never have. For example, we could load the whole junior and senior class on one Greyhound bus and take a school trip to Daytona Beach, Florida, which we did twice and had more fun than a circus bear.

In fact, the first time I ever got inebriated was on a school trip to Daytona Beach. I chug-a-lugged four beers, and the first thing I knew I was jumping up and down on the bed in the hotel room.

Another advantage was that they could bend the rules. Billy Hart and Bobby Jordan and me got a math credit for cleaning up the gym one period a day our senior year. Now, don't get me wrong. I'm not condoning the kind of educational process that allows a kid to get a year's math credit for goofing off. All I'm saying is, it worked. We turned out all right. Bobby Jordan retired from the Army after twenty years, Billy Hart is a successful businessman and I'm still trying to learn how to play this damn fiddle.

Graduation is a somber and lump-in-the-throat kind of time when you go to a small school, and that's how it was for the Goldston High Class of 1955. What do you say to people you've shared so much with? You know everybody, you know where they live, you know their brothers and sisters. You really *know* the person in that cap and gown. When there's only twenty-two people in your graduating class, it's almost like breaking up a family.

But that's what graduation is all about. It's time to cut old ties and get out in the world and pull your own weight, which I proceeded to do by going to work at the Cornell Dubilier factory in Sanford the week after I graduated. I was a general laborer for the company, which made electric capacitors.

Our band kept practicing, kept improving, and after a more successful audition we finally got our radio show. It was at six-thirty in the morning, each and every Saturday.

"Howdy, howdy, all you friends and neighbors out there in Radioland. It's time for The Misty Mountain Boys," was our intro. Then for half an hour we'd play bluegrass and country, borrowing often from Bill Monroe and Flatt and Scruggs.

After several months, we got our radio show moved to Saturday afternoon and even started playing a square dance once in a while at night. If we made five dollars each, we were delighted.

The band had changed by then. Joe Phillips had joined the Navy and Russell Palmer had taken over the banjo and was doing a good job at it. Ed Cooper was playing the doghouse bass and Dave Hall and then P.T. Wilkins played guitar for us. I was still sawing away on the fiddle.

Things were just starting to look up a little bit for The Misty Mountain Boys when my daddy changed jobs again and moved back to Wilmington. I was crushed this time. I really didn't want to go, but if my mama and daddy were moving, so was I.

I went to work with Daddy at the Taylor Colquitt Creosoting Company as an inspector. I kept on practicing on my instruments, but I couldn't find a band to play with. I went all around town talking to local musicians, but nobody wanted a chubby fiddle player.

One day a guitar player I knew, Billy Shepard, told me that a girl singer named "Little Jill" was looking for another guitar player for a steady job in a bar at Jacksonville (about fifty miles away). It paid fifty dollars a week for six nights. I tried out and got the job.

Just to be on the safe side, I kept my daytime job at Taylor Colquitt and drove to Jacksonville in the evening. I would get home about twelve-thirty or one o'clock, sleep a few hours and then get up about six-thirty or seven for my daytime job. I would sleep just about all day on Sundays. I'd usually get up late in the afternoon and go to a movie, and then the whole thing would start over again bright and early Monday morning.

The band consisted of Billy Shepard and myself on guitars, Little Jill on vocals and a guy named Steve on drums. I'd never played in a band with a drummer, and I really liked it. It added another dimension. We started doing a lot of rock-and-roll numbers, much to the delight of the customers who frequented Marvin's Western Bar.

Before long we got a new drummer, Tommy Clemmons, and added a bass player, Norman Tyson from Wilmington.

Charlie Daniels

Then Little Jill left the band, but we kept right on playing with me singing the lead vocals. We did real well at Marvin's Western Bar, but then Marvin got shut down for serving a minor or something, so we moved across the street to the S & M and continued to do real good business.

Our salaries had jumped up to eighty dollars a week, which was more than we were making on our daytime jobs. We were really clicking together. I worked pretty hard in those days — jumping around on stage, breaking guitar strings, but I was loving it.

Maybe my daytime job suffered a little bit because of my nighttime job, but all in all I managed to balance them pretty good. In the summer of 1958, business started slowing up for the Taylor Colquitt Creosoting Company to the point that they were going to have to lay somebody off in my department.

There were only two of us — myself and a man named Louis Frost. Louis knew twice as much about the job as I did. In fact, he had trained me. He also had been with the company a lot longer than I had, he worked harder than I did and he had a family to support. Oh, and one more thing — he was black.

Well, guess who they were going to lay off. Simply by virtue of my being born white, they were going to keep me and lay off Louis Frost.

I was pretty protective of my job — after all, I was the third generation of my family to work there — but I couldn't let that happen. So I went to the foreman and said, "Hell, lay me off instead of Louis. I've got a job playing music that pays eighty dollars a week."

Good sense finally prevailed. They kept Louis, who worked there until he retired a few years ago, and I went my way to chase a dream.

From that time on, I was a genuine, bona fide, professional musician.

And therein ends this story and begins another one. It's a story I intend to tell one of these days, but I don't feel that now is the time. I'm too busy living this story, and I've still got a lot of songs to write and sing and a lot of mountains to climb.

I will tell you this much, though. I have few regrets and I'm a very happy man. God has blessed me beyond my wildest expectations.

In this brief autobiography, I've tried to cover the time which corresponds to most of the stories I've written. The time when I was innately gathering material for this book.

I've tried to let you see the kind of life I lived during those formative years. I've known someone like most of the characters I've written about, and I've heard some good storytellers in my life and I'm sure they've had a profound effect on me.

I've played havoc with the geography and several other things concerning my home state of North Carolina in these stories, and I hope that the good people of the Tarheel state will forgive me.

A name or two is real, but most of my characters are totally fictitious. I guess some of them may be a little unusual, but I sure did enjoy inventing them.

This is my first attempt at anything literary, and I just sat down and wrote from my memory and my heart. I make no apologies for the grammatical errors, since I don't use good English when I talk. To me, words are meant to communicate with, proper or improper. And as long as you understand what I'm trying to say, I'm happy and grammar be hanged.

I only hope that you enjoy reading the following stories as much as I enjoyed writing them.

—CHARLIE DANIELS

The Devil Went Down to Georgia

THE DEVIL HADN'T been in Georgia in quite some time. He just didn't like the place to start with, and seeing as how things had been going along pretty good without him there, what with all the dry counties disappearing and Atlanta supplying so many people such a good opportunity to sin, he'd just stayed away.

But lately things had been slowing down in Georgia, and everywhere else for that matter, with Jim Bakker and Pat Robertson and all the rest of them satellite preachers booming down the airways all hours of the day and night. It was getting to the point that the devil had to fight for almost every soul he could get his hands on, and he still couldn't get much going.

It was a particularly beautiful day with the sun shining and the birds singing, the kind of a day that old devil just hated. In fact, he didn't care a whole lot for daylight anyway, preferring to do his work around midnight. But like I said, things had been slow, and here he was tromping around the Georgia countryside in a rotten frame of mind.

The reason for his rotten mood was that an old sinner he had been cultivating for years, and had already counted on having at the end of the year, had quit drinking, quit smoking, quit running around with women and had joined the Sand Springs Freewill Baptist Church and been baptized that very day. The devil just had to come to see for hisself. He almost couldn't believe it when the preacher had ducked old Brady Bullard under the water and he'd come up shouting, and since the devil had no power to interfere, he just had to watch helpless.

He was stomping down the side of the mountain, kicking up sparks, when he heard fiddle music drifting up the side of the hill. Now, just who would be playing a fiddle out here in the middle of nowhere? He rushed along to see.

He came to a little clearing, and lo and behold, there was this young feller sitting on a juniper log, sawing away on "Sally Gooden," and just as the devil got there, he switched over to "Ragtime Annie" and fairly made the bow dance across the strings.

The devil, knowing the reputation of fiddle players, got to thinking up a plan. An evil grin spread across his face as he stepped into the clearing.

"Well, hello there, boy. My, you do play that fiddle to a fare-thee-well. Do you know who I am?"

The boy set his fiddle aside and took a long, hard look. "From them pointed ears and that tail you're dragging behind you, I'd say you was probably a devil of some sort."

"A devil of some sort? Why, boy, you're not looking at *a* devil. I'm *the* Devil," snorted the devil, more than a little irritated at not being recognized by this belligerent hillbilly.

"Well, we don't need you around here, so you can just be on your way," the boy said as he tuned the E string on his fiddle.

"Boy, you'd better watch your mouth and show some respect." The devil was getting a little hot under the collar.

"I don't respect nobody that goes around with little horns on his head. You look like a billy goat, with that little goatee and all." And the boy started to snicker. That just infuriated the devil to no end, and he started flipping his tail back and forth, which was a nervous habit when he was upset.

"You've got a lot of nerve to be speaking to anybody in that fashion, standing out here in the middle of nowhere, screeching on a violin. Just a nobody in a straw hat. Who do you think you are?"

"In the first place, this ain't no violin. It's a fiddle. And as to who I am, I'm the best damn fiddle player in Monroe County, possibly the best damn fiddle player in Georgia. And maybe the best damn fiddle player in the world, that's who I am," the boy said, kinda proudlike.

The devil started laughing fit to be tied. "The best fiddle player in the world? Why, you're not even the best fiddle player in this miserable little clearing. I could outfiddle you myself on a one-string fiddle with one hand tied behind my back."

"You ain't even got a fiddle, you ugly old billy goat, and if you did, you still couldn't hold a candle to me," the boy said, laughing a little to hisself.

The devil snapped his fingers, and a fiddle case appeared in his hand. "Would you like to bet on that?" the devil said.

"I ain't got nothing to bet," the boy said. "This fiddle

belongs to my grandpa. But if I did have something, I'd sure bet with you, cause I'm the best there's ever been. But you might as well forget about it, cause I ain't got nothing to bet."

"Oh, I wouldn't say that," the devil said, kind of sly-like. "I'd be willing to take your soul."

"My soul? You must be crazy. I ain't gonna bet my soul against nothing."

"Not even this?" The devil snapped his fingers and a beautiful gold fiddle appeared in his hand. "Look at this, boy," the devil taunted.

The boy's eyes got big as silver dollars, and his mouth watered as he lusted for that gold fiddle.

"I might would for that if I was going to for anything, but I ain't gonna bet my soul," the boy said. But the devil could tell he was weakening.

"I'll tell you what, boy. I'll throw in this silver bow and this case made of the finest Moroccan leather and trimmed with diamonds. All that against one measly little soul. What do you say?"

The boy cast his eyes on that gold fiddle and that silver bow and that case crusted with diamonds, and the devil knew he had him.

"We ain't got nobody to judge," the boy said, trying real hard to keep from giving in.

"Why, we'll judge it ourselves," the devil said. "We both know good fiddle playing when we hear it. Come on." And he wiggled that gold fiddle so that the sun made it sparkle. It was just too much for the boy.

"All right," he said. "I mean to have that gold fiddle, cause like I said, I'm the best there's ever been."

"Done," the devil said before he could back out. "By

the way, what's your name, young man?"

"Johnny," the boy said.

"Well, Johnny, I'll go first," the devil said as he opened up his case and took a red fiddle out of it. He pulled a cake of rosin out of his pocket and started rosining up his bow, causing fire to fly.

The devil jumped up on a hickory stump and pulled the bow across the strings, and it sounded like a red-hot horseshoe dipped in a rain barrel — *HISSSSSSSSS*.

"Is that all you can do?" the boy said and started laughing.

"Just stand back, boy," the devil said and started fiddling "The Devil's Dream" real fast. After a couple of choruses, he switched into something that sounded like a thousand witches screaming, and then the demons started popping up playing instruments. There were little demons in the treetops playing flutes and piccolos. There were great big demons on the ground playing bass fiddles and big bass drums. There were demons of every size and description playing hell-for-leather on all manner of instruments. And the devil stood on that hickory stump in the middle of it all with smoke coming off his bow, sawing like . . . well, like the devil.

The devil and his band of demons played and played. The wind started blowing and it rained, then it snowed, and then it hailed and the ground started shaking and the trees trembled. The noise was so deafening that the boy had to shut his eyes and put his fingers in his ears.

One last ear-splitting crescendo and then it was over. The smoke cleared and the demons disappeared, and there stood the devil putting his fiddle back in his case.

"You might as well give up right now, boy," the devil

said. "You know you can't beat that."

"Like hell I will," the boy said. "You've had your say, now sit down over there and let me have mine. You play pretty good, but I'm gonna show you how it's done."

The boy stood up and raised his fiddle to his chin and played "Maiden's Prayer" so pretty it would break your heart. Then he lit into "Buffalo Gals," and then he was off and running. "Bile Them Cabbage Down, Bake Them Hoecakes Brown," "Fire on the Mountain, Run Boys Run," "Chicken in the Bread Pan, Picking Out Dough, Granny Does Your Dog Bite, No Child No," "Girls on Cripple Creek Bout Half Grown, Jump on a Man Like a Dog on a Bone," "Birdie in the Cage," "Alamand Left With a Right and Left Hand," "Swing Your Partner Round and Round," "Cotton-Eyed Joe and Bully of the Town," "Old Joe Clark, Black Mountain Rag, Way Down Yonder and Slewfoot Drag."

Then he went into "Orange Blossom Special," and I'll swear, you could hear that train rolling down the track just as plain as day. He sawed the hair right off the bow and kept right on playing with the bow stick.

The devil never had heard such fiddle playing in a thousand years. He started patting his foot and then got up and started doing a fancy buck and wing. "Shave and Haircut," and it was all over. The devil was plumb out of breath.

The boy put the fiddle back in the case, and the devil looked at him trying to pretend that he wasn't impressed.

"You lose," the devil said, but he didn't say it with much conviction.

"Like hell I do," the boy said. "Like I told you, I'm the best there's ever been."

The devil argued for a while, but it was no use. He knew he had lost fair and square.

He laid the gold fiddle at the boy's feet and said, "How about double or nothing?"

The boy laughed and picked up the gold fiddle and pulled the silver bow across the strings.

"Well, would you at least play "Fire on the Mountain" one more time?" the devil said, kind of dejectedlike.

And the boy did, and the devil danced. And when it was over, the boy went home, and the devil went to New Orleans for a poker game with a gambler who was about to cash in.

Radio Smith

ME AND ED SIMPSON and Elmer Suggs and a feller named Radio Smith (his real name was Calvin Smith, but everybody called him Radio because he talked all the time) was out fishing over on Cedar Creek when we seen the biggest catfish any of us had ever seen.

At first I thought Elmer had hung on to a rock or something, the way his pole bent. And then I seen this head come up out of the water, and that mouth was big enough to swallow a cantaloupe. His whiskers was about the size of a twenty-penny nail, and he must have weighed about fifty pounds. He was thrashing around and carrying on and was full of fight.

We was just fishing for crappie and using real light tackle, so Elmer never had a chance. That line popped like a .22 rifle, and there was a big splash and that rascal was long gone.

Poor old Elmer sat down on a stump and cussed for five minutes.

Ed Simpson said, "That's the biggest son of a buck I've every seen." What Ed meant was, "son of a bitch," but Ed was a Baptist, so he said, "son of a buck."

Elmer said, "Damn that piece of banjo-bellied, pigeon-toed, knock-kneed, snaggle-toothed, crippled-dick, cheap-ass, son-of-a-bitching line." Elmer was a Methodist.

I said, "Elmer, it won't but four-pound test. Hell, that big bull must have weighed fifty or sixty pounds."

"I don't give a big rat's ass if it was *three*-pound test. Why did the dadblamed thing have to bust when I had ahold of the biggest catfish in the state of North Carolina, probably the biggest catfish in the world? Give me another beer."

Then Radio Smith lit in. Now, you'd have to hear this feller to believe it. I mean, he could change subjects in the middle of a sentence and never miss a gear. Anyway, he said, "Elmer, what you ought to a-done was to a-played him to the bank on top of the water. I remember one time me and Grady Sykes was fishing down on the Santee and I hooked an alligator, and he pulled us down the river for about three miles. He must have had that boat going twenty-five miles an hour, and Grady Sykes fell out of the boat and caught pneumonia and damn near died. I tell you when that was. It was the same year that Wiley Parsons killed that eight-point buck, except it won't no eight-point buck, it was a seven-point buck. I seen the damn thing. He was showing it off up at Harold Jessup's filling station. Did you know that Harold Jessup was putting in one a them little biddy pool tables? I'm pretty good on them little biddy pool tables. I remember one time I won five dollars off of Burton Seagroves. It made him madder than hell. You know, Burton always did get pissed off real easy. I seen Harmon Blocker tear his ass up and down at the VFW one night. It was over that girl that stayed with Mrs. Binkley last summer, you know. . . ."

"Radio, if you don't shut up, I'm gonna ram this beer can down your throat!" Elmer Suggs hollered.

"Well, you don't have to be so jawdy about it, Elmer. You remind me of Amos Gillespie. Amos Gillespie was the jawdiest man I ever seen. You know my uncle practically raised Amos. His daddy run him off when he won't but sixteen years old. Caught him messing around with Mrs. Ava Gunter's daughter. . . ."

"Radio, you son of a bitch, if you say another word, I'm gonna break your neck. Now, shut up. S-H-U-T U-P!"

"I can spell, Elmer. I was good in school. In fact, I made straight A's in the third grade in Mrs. Wonble's room. You know, she's seventy years old and still teaching, teaches the three R's: readin', 'riting, and 'rithmetic. That's all the people really need, the three R's. If a man can read and write and figure, he can do a right fair job of anything. Now, you take Johnny Farmer. He's been to college and he's a fool, a educated fool. He don't know his ass from a hole in the ground. . . ."

Elmer Suggs screamed like a wildcat and grabbed ahold of Radio Smith's neck, and it took me and Ed Simpson both to prize him off of him.

"I'm sorry, Radio," Elmer said as soon as me and Ed had pulled him off. "I guess I'm a little upset about losing that catfish."

Well, Radio was being big-hearted about it. He said, "Oh, that's all right, Elmer, I know what it's like to lose something. I lost my pocket watch last year. The one that Papa give me. You know, he had that old watch for forty years. He got it in Rockingham when he worked for the Atlantic Coastline Railroad. You know, there ain't no Atlantic Coastline Railroad no more. It's the Seaboard Coastline Railroad now. Got the main office in Jacksonville, Florida. I went down there one time with the twelfth grade. Stayed in a hotel. First nineteen-cent hamburger place I ever seen was right next door to it. I eat fourteen of them things and got sick. Sick as a dog. . . ."

After you've been around Radio Smith for a while, you get to where you figure that he's part of the background noise, like the crickets chirping or the birds singing. So you just go and carry on conversations with other people and just ignore Radio. Hell, he don't care. He just keeps on jabbering.

Anyway, Elmer said, "I'm gonna catch that catfish. I'm gonna fish till I catch him, and then I'm gonna carry him uptown and make that smart-ass Vernon Savage so damn jealous he can't stand it. He makes me sick every since he caught that eight-pound bass, bragging and carrying on all the time. I'm gonna catch that big son of a bitch."

"Hell, I'd like to catch that big son of a bitch myself," Ed Simpson said, forgetting about being a Baptist for a minute.

"As long as it ain't Vernon Big-Ass Savage, I don't care who catches him," Elmer said.

After a minute, Ed said, "Now, I wouldn't care much about Tyree Mullins catching him. He already thinks that he's the best-looking son of a buck in town."

Well, everybody agreed on that, and the conversation stopped for a minute.

We could hear Radio Smith in the background, "And I told him, I said, I can't be responsible for your collard greens. I do well to tend mine. I ain't got time to do nothing else. I ain't even got time to go fishing no more. You know, I'm gonna start taking some time off. I was thinking about going to Myrtle Beach this year, but I may go to the Darlington 500. I been to Daytona. . . ."

"What do you think he'd bite the best on?"

"Hell, I was fishing a cricket in about three feet of water. I've never heard of a catfish biting a cricket."

"I've heard of it, but not too often."

"I believe I'd try some chicken livers."

"You know, them big old night crawler worms might be the thing."

Well, everybody stopped and thought about that.

That is, everybody but Radio. ". . . was driving Mr. Rayford Liggin's John Deere tractor, just clean pulled it out of the ditch. It was that great big curve up past Patterson's barn — you know, the one that burnt down. They said he set that barn on fire. Papa knew a man in Pittsboro one time that burnt down his own outhouse. They called the fire department and. . . ."

"Reckon what pound test a feller ought to use?"

"The heaviest thing you can get around here is about twenty-pound test. Anything heavier than that would be saltwater, and you'd have to go to the coast to get that."

"I'll tell you what, I'll bet you. I'll bet you that a man could get one a them big hooks and use some a that clothesline, and put a big chunk of chicken liver on it, and fish real hard and catch that big joker."

Food for thought.

Radio was still at it. "And she won't but nineteen years old, and after that he won't worth a durn. It kinda reminds me of the time that me and Horton Collie got lost back in the flat woods, and Horton said, 'Calvin,' he said, 'if you know the way home, why don't you take us on out?' Well, right about then I seen this great big cypress tree. . . ."

"You know, I got a good mind to take off work next week and catch that big sucker."

"You know, that ain't a bad idea. I could take a week of my vacation."

"I wonder how a feller would do fishing for him at night. Catfish feed at night, too."

". . . put the son of a bitch in jail. He ended up doing thirty days, and you know, when he come out of jail, he straightened up and worked hard and bought that little beer joint across from the Dairy Queen. I was in there one night and these two fellers got into it over who got the pool table next. You know, I don't even like them big old regulation pool tables. I like them little biddy pool tables. You know, I'm pretty good on one a them little biddy pool tables. . . ."

"I'll bet you they'd be some kind of a prize for catching a catfish that size."

"I hear that feller that caught that big small-mouth last year won a new bass rig and all kinda stuff."

"Damn, I'd sure love to have me a new bass rig. Uh huh!"

". . . so, Papa just left him standing there all night long. Papa told him, 'If you're gonna dance, you gotta pay the fiddler,' did you ever hear . . . Ohmigosh! Ohmigosh! Hell, oh hell! Damnation! Son of a bitch!"

Radio Smith's pole was bent double, and his line was as taut as a fiddle string. Radio had a monster on the line.

Everybody was hollering advice at Radio: "Don't give him no slack, Radio!"

"Play him up close to the bank, Radio!"

And Radio was battling away ninety miles an hour. "Damn! Damn! Oh, hell! Big fish, come up here on the hill, you wall-eyed son of a bitch."

Radio Smith almost lost that fish three different times, but somehow or other he hung on and landed a whopping big bass. I mean, this sucker was big. We threw him in the back of Elmer Suggs's pickup and took off for town, straight to Harold Jessup's Filling Station. It was about three o'clock on a Saturday afternoon, and the town was loaded down with people.

Well, of all the people to be hanging around Harold Jessup's Filling Station, Vernon Savage and Tyree Mullins were both there. We pulled up in front of the full-service pump, and the word spread up and down the street like wildfire. "Biggest bass you've ever seen down at Harold Jessup's Filling Station."

"Who caught him?"

"Radio Smith."

"Well, I'll be damned!"

"I believe he's bigger than that one that Vernon Savage caught last year."

"What did he catch him on?"

"Crickets."

We took the bass and weighed him on the meat scales at Melvin Potter's Butcher Shop, and he weighed eight pounds and four ounces. It outweighed Vernon Savage's fish by four ounces.

Well, Vernon Savage and Tyree Mullins didn't even come out of the inside of Harold Jessup's Filling Station. They acted like they didn't even know what was going on. They just kept ignoring us. Finally Harold Jessup stepped inside and said, "You boys ought to come out and look at this fish before they take it away."

Well, you could tell that they didn't like it much, but they walked up to Elmer's truck and looked at him. Finally Tyree said, kind of matter-of-factly, "Who caught him?"

"Radio Smith."

Vernon Savage said, "You've got to be joking. What did he do, talk him to death?" And him and Tyree Mullins laughed real loud, but they was the only ones that laughed.

About that time Radio stepped up and said, "Hey, Vernon. Hey, Tyree. Big fish, ain't it? Weighs more than that one you caught last year, Vernon. Caught him on a cricket. I usually fish with worms. I dig 'em up out of Harvey Nester's cow lot, out there next to where he keeps that big Santa Gertrudis Bull. You got to watch that boy; he'll hook the hell out of you, if he gets a chance. He puts me in the mind of that old bull that Mr. Marvin Russ used to keep over back of Papa's pasture. You couldn't get within a hundred yards of that rascal. I mean, he went for anything that moved. Me and my cousin Murray was coming through back there one day, and Murray had stuck a nail in his foot and couldn't run worth a durn. You know, he finally got lockjaw from that nail. Stayed in the hospital up in Lumberton for two weeks. He was some kinda sick, he was. . . ."

Harold Jessup stepped up and said, "Radio, let me buy you boys a Co-Cola," and he did buy a Co-Cola for me and Ed and Elmer, and he give one to Radio, but he never did drink his. He was too busy talking.

Anyway, what I meant to bring out was, it kinda meant something to have old Harold Jessup buy you a Co-Cola. Not that he's stingy or nothing like that, but Harold just generally bought one for fellers that caught the biggest fish or killed the buck with the biggest rack. Or like when our high school boys won a game, he'd buy them all one.

We was plain-out celebrities, specially Radio since he caught that bass, and me and Ed and Elmer cause we was there when it happened.

Well, in a little while Carl Willets kinda sidled up to me and says, "Hey, old son, don't you want something in that Coke besides Coke?"

Well, me and him and Ed and Elmer stepped out in the grease rack and had us a good pull of Jim Beam. Gilbert Johnson had a pint of Early Times in his truck, and us same three had a snort of that.

We was getting all kinds of attention. Oh, by the way, it wasn't because they didn't like Radio, the reason they didn't offer him a drink. The truth is, you just don't give Radio Smith whiskey. I mean, he just couldn't drink. You could hit him in the ass with a rotten apple and he was drunk. But I seen him drunk one time and he tried to fight everybody in the whole place, including a Salvation Army woman standing outside the door taking up a collection.

Well, anyway, we was getting the major part of the attention. Somebody give Radio a cigar and he never did light it, but he chewed that thing all to pieces.

Boy, I tell you, we was in the middle of things and you could see that it was killing Vernon Savage and Tyree Mullins. I mean, they won't used to this. Vernon Savage was the big fisherman in our part of the county, and to hear Tyree tell it, he had deflowered every female between here and Fayetteville. One of them was talking fishing and one of them was talking women all the time. Vernon Savage had a bass rig with a trolling motor on the side, and Tyree

Charlie Daniels

Mullins had a new Trans Am with a pack of Trojans in the glove compartment. Anyway, both of them was always spouting off like nobody else in the county knew anything about fishing or fornicating.

There must have been twenty-five or thirty people standing around talking when somebody said, "Well, I reckon you're gonna have him mounted, ain't you?"

And Radio said, "Hell no, I ain't gonna have him mounted. I'm gonna eat him."

Well, Vernon Savage jumped in and said kinda smartlike, "Nobody but a fool would eat a bass that big," and Tyree Mullins snickered.

"Well, I don't give a damn what a fool would do. I'm gonna eat this joker. Besides, I ain't got no place to hang him if I did get him mounted. I'd have to put him up over the mantelpiece, and I'd have to take down that picture of Mama and Papa, and I couldn't do that. It was the picture they had made the day they got married, the one with Papa in that long-tailed suit. You know, I've still got that old suit. They don't make clothes now-a-days like they did back then. Course, they don't make nothing like they used to. You take my new pickup truck. I took it back to the shop three times. I told Wayne, I said, 'I want you to fix this thing. I'm getting tired of bringing it up here.' Well, he got it to where it runs all right, but that thing won't go by a gas station without stopping. I mean it eats the gas."

Radio had to stop and grab a quick breath, and I jumped in and said that I thought Radio had done a good job of landing that big son of a gun, and Ed said that he thought he'd done a good job of landing that big son of a buck, too.

Well, Vernon Savage upped and said, "I don't know why you're making so much out of it. Hell, he was just

56

plain lucky. He'll never do it again in his whole life."

Now, that just kinda pissed me off, and I've always been a little loose-mouthed when I had me a drink or two of good whiskey. Anyway, I said, "I bet you a hundred dollars that he can outfish you any day of the week."

That smart-ass Tyree Mullins jumped up then and said, "You're covered," and then the betting started, and before long everybody in the room had something bet on Vernon Savage or Radio Smith.

We decided to get Harold Jessup to hold the money and keep it in his safe at the filling station. All told, it was about fifteen hundred dollars.

That was about five o'clock in the afternoon, and by the time Harold closed up at ten o'clock that night, he had over four thousand dollars in his safe.

They said that on Monday a feller came by and said he'd heard about it clear over at Evergreen, and he wanted to put fifty dollars on Vernon Savage. When Harold Jessup took the money over to the bank Thursday for safekeeping, he had a little over eleven thousand dollars. The odds were running ten to one for Vernon Savage.

Harold Jessup said that he'd give a tank full of gas and a case of Co-Cola's to the winner. And Mr. Jacobs at the hardware store said he'd give the winner a case of twelve-gauge shotgun shells, and the Dairy Queen said that the winner could eat there free every Tuesday night for a year.

We decided, or rather Vernon Savage decided (he claimed that he'd fished in more tournaments than anybody else and that he knew how they was supposed to work) that him and Radio would both fish Cedar Creek and start at five o'clock in the morning and weigh the fish in at five o'clock in the evening.

One thing that Vernon didn't get was he just wanted to count large-mouth bass. We said, "No deal. We count any kind of fish and any size of fish. Overall poundage will decide the winner."

They was gonna do it next Saturday if it won't raining, and I decided that I'd better protect my investment, so I took off over to Radio's house. When I got there, Ed Simpson and Elmer Suggs were already there.

Elmer said, "Radio, we got to get your tackle and bait together. They tell me that Vernon Savage has got every bass plug known to man, and he's got a live well for minnows, and he carries night crawlers and crickets. What you figuring on fishing with, Radio?"

"I figure on fishing with the same thing I caught that big bass with. I feel downright lucky about fishing with crickets. Yeah, I got this here lucky feeling. I got that feeling one night at the fair when I was playing bingo, and I bingo'd three times. I won two thermos bottles and a checkerboard. I've still got the checkerboard. . . ."

"Wait a minute! Wait a minute, Radio! You mean to tell me that all you're gonna fish with is crickets! Hot damn, man! Vernon Savage has got a depth-finder and a trolling motor and all that bait, and all you're gonna fish with is damn crickets? You're crazy as hell!"

"You don't have to holler, Elmer. I told you I got a lucky feeling about them crickets, and I don't need all that other stuff anyhow, cause I won't be in no boat. I just don't like riding in boats. They make me feel queasy at my stomach. You know, I get that same way if I eat a bate of dried apples, I just have to. . . ."

Elmer's face turned red and I thought he'd swallowed his tongue, and me and Ed grabbed ahold of him just in case.

"Radio Smith, you're the dumbest, most ignorant, dim-witted, sawdust-headed, aggravating son of a bitch I ever seen in my life. You can't sit up on the bank and catch any fish. You've got to get out in a boat and go find them this time of year."

"Elmer, I don't care what you say, I ain't going out in no boat. I'm gonna win, and I'm gonna sit right on the bank and I ain't even gonna take a dinner break. I'm gonna carry my lunch and eat it right there on the bank and keep right on fishing. I'll guarantee you I'm gonna win. I was saying to somebody the other day, I said, 'I'm gonna go down there to that creek and I'm gonna whip Vernon Savage like a two-dollar mule. . . .'"

Well, Elmer just turned around and went and got in his truck and slammed the door and took off squealing tires. He was some kinda pissed off.

Me and Ed stayed around for the biggest part of the day trying to talk some sense into Radio's hard head, but I might as well a-been talking to my brood sow, for all the good it done.

"But Radio, you don't understand. There ain't no fish up next to the bank this time of year."

But Radio could be the stubbornest feller I ever seen in my life. "I ain't getting in no boat. I feel the same way about getting in a boat that I feel about getting on a Ferris wheel. I got sick on a Ferris wheel over at Lumberton and threw up on the feller running it. That same night Byron Ballard spent twenty-five dollars throwing baseballs at them little puppy dog sort of things, trying to win a teddy bear for Beth Ann. He told that feller, he said, 'I believe y'all got a wire hooked up behind them things to keep 'em from falling. . . .'"

Well, me and Ed seen that we might as well a-been trying to stuff a hoe handle up a hummingbird's ass. After a while we just give up.

I tell you, a hundred dollars is a lot of money to me, and I never felt more like a fool than I did watching Vernon Savage taking off in that Cadillac outfit of his, and watching Radio Smith sitting down on the bank with that cane pole and that pitiful little box of crickets.

And then the first thing he done is he left the lid off the cricket box and all the crickets got out. He couldn't manage to catch but three of them, so me and Elmer hauled ass up to the crossroads and got three more boxes of crickets.

Well, we was gone about thirty minutes, and when we got back, Radio Smith hadn't had a bite. Vernon Savage had a CB radio on his boat, and he had called somebody and said that he'd caught a three-pound bass.

Radio changed the cricket on his hook and said, "They kinda slow biting today, ain't they! But they'll get started after a while. It takes anything some time to get started. Why, when I get up in the morning, it takes me a few minutes to get awake. I generally get up about 5:30, you know. It's clean daylight that time of the morning. It's the best part of the day. I like to get up and eat breakfast. You know what I like for breakfast once in a while? Catfish. I love catfish for breakfast. . . ."

"Well, damn if you ain't gonna starve to death tomorrow morning," Elmer said.

It was twelve o'clock and my belly was starting to growl, and Radio still hadn't had a bite. I drove up to the Dairy Queen and got some hot dogs, and when I got back Radio Smith had caught a fish — a bluegill that probably weighed about a half pound.

Somebody said that Vernon had called in and said that he'd caught a four-pound rock fish, trolling.

Well, about three o'clock that evening I finally had to admit what I'd known for a week: I was gonna lose my hundred dollars. There wasn't nothing I could do about it, but I damn sure didn't have to face it sober. So me and Ed and Elmer drove over to town to get some beer. When we got back, Radio had caught another bluegill that mighta weighed a pound.

Then all of a sudden, his cork went under. Radio brought it up and it was about a five-pound carp, the only fish in the creek that didn't count. Oh, then he got hot catching carp. He musta-caught about ten in a row, and then they stopped and he didn't get another bite for an hour.

Somebody come up and said that Vernon Savage had caught about forty pounds of bass and rock fish and that he was quitting because his arm had got tired and that he was on his way in.

Well, Vernon come riding up in that fancy boat of his and they commenced to take fish off that thing, and I didn't think they'd ever quit. He had fourteen bass and rock fish that weighed in at forty-three pounds.

It was a quarter till five and everybody was gathered around Vernon Savage, beating him on the back and offering him drinks of whiskey, and Radio Smith fished on. When it was five minutes till five, I walked down to where Radio was and said, "You might as well give up and come on up here. It's almost five o'clock."

"I'm gonna win, I'm gonna win. I got this here lucky feeling when I was catching them carp while ago. I could tell that they was gonna bite right before they did. You know, most people won't eat a carp, but they don't know how to fix it. You got to get you a good piece of pine wood and cut that mud vein out of the carp and lay him on that pine, and take some pepper and red onions and . . . Ohmigosh! Ohmigosh! Oh, hell! Oh, damn!"

That cane pole was bent to the snapping point and just about to break, and I seen this head come up out of the water. I recognized it right away — mouth big enough to swallow a cantaloupe, whiskers about the size of a twenty-penny nail, and thrashing around and carrying on for all he was worth.

Radio Smith grabbed the line just before the pole broke, and that fish was dragging him around on the bank. Radio dug his heels into the ground and started pulling that fish in hand-over-hand. Radio fought a good fight and got him on the bank just as somebody hollered that it was five o'clock.

He was a buffalo catfish, the same one that Elmer Suggs had hooked, because he still had a piece of Elmer's line hanging out of his mouth.

We was mighty excited as we drug him up the hill to the scales, but when they weighed him it took the wind out of our sails. He weighed forty-two pounds and eight ounces. He was one-half pound less than Vernon's whole catch. Damn the luck.

Vernon Savage and Tyree Mullins had smirks on their faces, and I just wanted to jump in the creek. I knew we'd never live this down.

"Wait a minute! Wait a minute!" Radio Smith hollered, and he went running back down to the creek and pulled out a stringer full of carp and ran back up the hill with them. Tyree Mullins stepped up and said, "Hey, dumb-ass, carp don't count."

"I know it," Radio said, unstringing the carp. "I almost forgot about these little fellers." And he dropped the two little bluegills on the scale. They pushed the scale to forty-three and three-quarters pounds!

"I win! I win!" Radio hollered. "I told you I was gonna win. I knew I was gonna win. You didn't believe me, did you? I win! I win! I win!"

"Shut up, you damn idiot!" Vernon Savage was fit to be tied. "He can't do that! He can't throw them baby blue-gills on there and win!"

"Vernon, we said all fish, old son, don't you remember?"

"Yeah, but hell, them ain't even fish!"

"You better bet your ass they're fish, and them damn sure count!"

Well, everybody had to agree. We'd said all fish counted (except carp), and them little bluegills were just as much fish as them big bass Vernon caught.

But Tyree Mullins stepped up and said, "I say that the son of a bitch is wrong, and anybody that don't like it will have to walk over the top of me to get my money."

Tyree Mullins never should have said that. I don't mean that Tyree ain't bad — he's kicked a whole bunch of asses in our part of the country — but he ain't never seen the day that he could handle Elmer Suggs.

Elmer just stepped up and kicked the unadulterated slop out of Tyree Mullins. Tyree was lying on the ground rubbing his jaw and saying, "Elmer Suggs, you son of a bitch, you sucker-punched me. You hit me from the blind side!"

Well, Elmer reached down and picked him up by the

collar and said, "Well, you take a good look this time, cause here it comes again," and he popped him in the other jaw. Tyree didn't say nothing that time.

We loaded Radio's big catfish on Elmer's truck and headed for Harold Jessup's Filling Station. When we pulled up, everybody started cheering and all. You'd a-thought that we was the football team coming out on the field.

Harold got the money out and paid the winners off, and Rhyford Lawson broke out a half a gallon of Brunswick County whiskey. It was sugar whiskey made in a copper still, and the best-tasting stuff you ever put in your mouth.

Vernon Savage finally drove up. He'd had to take Tyree Mullins over to the emergency room and get his mouth sewed up. They looked like whipped puppies and was real nice to everybody.

I said, "Radio, I reckon you thought you was gonna lose, going right down to the wire like that and all."

"Well, I'll tell you, it's like this. I never did have no doubts about winning. Papa used to tell me I could do anything I wanted to. Well, not everything. I've always wanted to go to Disneyland and I ain't never been there. You know, that's way out in California, out there where they grow oranges on trees. I don't like oranges, but I love apples and pecans. Mama used to bake this chocolate cake with pecans in it, and mister, I can tell you it was some kinda good. Make your tongue slap your eyeballs out. I think I'm gonna have that son of a bitch mounted. . . ."

Mrs. Eloise

MRS. ELOISE CONYERS had a headache every day of her life, or at least she claimed she did. She'd walk down to Higgins's Grocery Store every day. "Bobby, give me a BC and a Co-Cola. My head's just about to split."

Then it got to be two times a day, then three times a day, and then poor old Mrs. Eloise's head got to hurting so bad that she had to stay home full-time and drink Cokes and take headache powders all day long.

Bobby Higgins used to deliver the soft drinks and headache powders along with her grocery order.

On account of professional ethics, Bobby never would say how much he took up there, but he would admit that it was considerable.

Due to her humongous intake of soft drinks and lying around in bed all day, Mrs. Eloise got as big as the side of a house. Then she developed sinus trouble, fallen arches, liver trouble, a heart murmur, a kidney disorder and a host of other diseases that have not found their way into the medical books to this day.

I guess that you could say that Mrs. Eloise made a profession out of being sick. She took handfuls of patent medicine and anything else that she could talk Dr. Mercison out of.

Mrs. Eloise nearly died three or four times a week, which suited the ladies of the Baptist Sunshine Auxiliary just fine, since they could sit by her deathbed and commiserate about their own aches and pains.

"Maxine, I tell you, my head hurt so bad yesterday morning that I thought it was gonna bust. And then my liver got to acting up at the same time. I tell you, I thought my time had come."

"I know, Eloise. It was the same way with me when I had my pancreas attack last week. I told Dr. Simon, I said, 'Dr. Simon, if you can't give me something for the pain, just put me out of my misery. Just put me out of my misery!' And you know, Eloise, all he'd give me was this little biddy pill, and it didn't do me one blessed bit of good."

"What color of a pill was it, Maxine?"

"Pink."

"I bet you it's the same one that Dr. Mercison gives me for my menstrual cramps. They don't do me no good either."

"Eloise, did you hear about Blanche Fletcher?"

"No."

"Well, you know, she's going in the hospital next Thursday. The doctor says that he's just going to remove her gallstones, but Blanche says that she figures that it's probably cancer or something like that."

"Well, that's where I need to be at, in the hospital,

Maxine. I just don't know how much longer I can keep going. I tell you, it's a pure trial just getting through the day."

"Eloise, I hope you get to feeling better. I've got to go. I'm meeting Beth and Martha, and we're gonna go by Blanche's for a while. The poor thing is just so sick."

After Maxine left, Mrs. Eloise got so mad that she jumped out of bed and stomped around the room for a half hour. How dare that Blanche Fletcher steal her thunder. Cancer indeed! She probably didn't even have gallstones.

But it looked as if Blanche Fletcher was about to receive the ultimate status symbol. A surgery scar was big business with the ladies of the Baptist Sunshine Auxiliary, and Mrs. Eloise had never even had an ingrown toenail removed.

Mrs. Eloise was sorely depressed. Hardly anybody came by to see her anymore. They were all going by to see Blanche Fletcher. What fun was it being sick when you didn't have a soul around to tell about it? How could fate be so cruel?

Mrs. Eloise's sister came to visit her for a few days, and life took on meaning again. The only trouble was that Mrs. Eloise had a hard time getting a word in edgewise, since her sister was just about as sick as she was.

"Polly, I've got this feeling inside of me that medicine just don't do no good. I don't think I'm long for this world."

"Where does it hurt you at, Eloise?"

"Oh, it just hurts all over. It just feels like my insides is all knotted up."

"It sounds to me like what you need is a complete hysterectomy."

"A what?"

"A complete hysterectomy."

"What does that do?"

"Well, they cut you along here and up under here and take out all your female parts."

"Well, do tell."

The more Polly talked, the more appealing a complete hysterectomy sounded to Mrs. Eloise.

By the time her sister went back to Tampa, Mrs. Eloise had decided that a complete hysterectomy was the only way in the world that she could survive.

One day when her husband got home from work, she said, "Melvin, I want you to call Dr. Mercison and tell him that I want a complete hysterectomy tomorrow morning."

"A what?"

"A complete hysterectomy."

"I didn't know you had hemorrhoids."

"No, you idiot, it's an operation on your female parts. They cut them out."

"You mean they're gonna whack your titties off?"

"Melvin, if my lumbago didn't hurt so bad, I'd get out of this bed and smack you right upside of the head. Now, get on that phone and call Dr. Mercison right this minute!"

If Melvin won't henpecked, he was mighty close to it. He was scared to death of Mrs. Eloise.

"Hello, Dr. Mercison. How are you? Fine, thank you. Hey listen, my wife needs a complete history on her rectum. . . . Just a minute, Doc. Eloise, he says there ain't nothing wrong with your rectum."

Mrs. Eloise finally had to drag her poor old pain-wracked body out of bed and talk to the doctor.

"Dr. Mercison, I need a complete hysterectomy."

"How do you know you need a complete hysterectomy, Mrs. Conyers?"

"My sister, Polly, said that was just what I needed."

"Is your sister a doctor?"

"No, she's not."

"Well, Mrs. Conyers, that may not be what you need at all. You may be having cramps."

"No, doctor, it ain't the cramps. I've had the cramps before. No, it ain't the cramps. I need a complete hysterectomy, and I'll do good to last out tomorrow without one."

Just to get off the phone, Dr. Mercison agreed to see her the next day.

That night Mrs. Eloise had a dream. She was at the weekly meeting of the Baptist Sunshine Auxiliary, and that busybody Blanche Fletcher was bragging about having her gallstones removed.

In the dream, Mrs. Eloise had stood up and said, "I've just had a complete hysterectomy." Blanche Fletcher had gasped and Clarabelle Johnson had just fell out on the floor.

She still had a warm feeling when she woke up the next morning.

She made Melvin drive her to Dr. Mercison's office, complaining about her female parts all the way. Dr. Mercison examined her and declared that she needed a complete hysterectomy about as much as she needed her nose cut off. Probably less.

Mrs. Eloise got so upset that she had one of her famous fainting spells right there on the floor of Dr. Mercison's office. Dr. Mercison just walked out of the room and left her lying there. Mrs. Eloise got over her fainting spell in record time and followed Dr. Mercison around the office.

"Why can't I have a complete hysterectomy? Other women have complete hysterectomies. Why can't I have one?"

"For the last time, Mrs. Conyers, I'm not going to give you a hysterectomy. You don't need one. Now, that's final."

"Very well, if you won't give me one, I'll go see Dr. Simon. He'll give me one."

Dr. Mercison had been putting up with Mrs. Eloise for a lot of years, and he just finally got fed up.

"Damn it, woman, I've never seen anyone want to be sick so bad. There's not a confounded thing wrong with you, except that you lie around on your fat ass all day long drinking those infernal soft drinks. What you need is a good diet and some exercise."

Mrs. Eloise was so shocked that she had another fainting spell and stayed out considerably longer this time.

She was as good as her word, though, and the next day she made Melvin drive her to Dr. Simon's office.

Dr. Simon also refused to give her a complete hysterectomy, so the next day she made Melvin drive her to see a doctor in the next county. He also refused.

Mrs. Eloise was getting depressed again, and to make matters worse, Blanche Fletcher had just got out of the hospital from her gallstone operation and was the toast of the Baptist Sunshine Auxiliary.

Mrs. Eloise went back to Dr. Mercison, who still refused to operate on her but did agree to take her back as a patient. There was one bright spot for her, though. Dr. Mercison said that she had a bona fide case of varicose veins.

But what are varicose veins compared to a complete hysterectomy? Mrs. Eloise knew that she could never be happy without one.

She made Melvin drive her to Atlanta, and after trying five doctors, she finally found one who agreed to give her a complete hysterectomy.

Mrs. Eloise was overjoyed. She couldn't wait to get back home and tell the girls.

She waddled into the weekly meeting of the Baptist Sunshine Auxiliary where Blanche Fletcher was basking in the glory of her gallstone operation. Mrs. Eloise casually mentioned that she had just got back from Atlanta.

"Well, what on earth were you doing in Atlanta, Eloise?"

"I went to see a doctor."

"A specialist?"

"A surgeon."

"Well, what did he say about you?"

"He said that I needed a complete hysterectomy in the worst kind of way," Mrs. Eloise blurted out, her voice rising so that Blanche Fletcher would be sure to hear all the way across the room.

"Well, you poor thing," Cora Potter said enviously.

"Yes, he said my female parts are in the worst shape you ever did see. Said he'd have to operate on me no later than next week. I'll probably be in the hospital for a month."

Blanche Fletcher was getting irritated at Mrs. Eloise's instant celebrity, and besides, she'd only been in the hospital for a week with her gallstone operation. She said, "I'm surprised that he'll operate on you, as fat as you are, Eloise."

"Well, he is, and I'd thank you to keep your medical

opinions to yourself, Blanche Fletcher. After all, you only had a piddling little gallstone operation. That don't amount to nothing."

"You got a lot of nerve to say that, Eloise Conyers. Why, I almost had cancer."

"Ha! And another thing — you've got the ugliest scar I've ever seen."

"Well, I never. Dr. Simon said that I had one of the neatest scars he'd ever sewed up."

"That don't surprise me none. What kind of a doctor is he anyway? He didn't even know that I needed a complete hysterectomy."

And so it went, all the bitchy little words that make up female one-upsmanship.

The big day finally arrived, and Mrs. Eloise had her best nightgowns packed. She made Melvin borrow his brother's station wagon and put a mattress in the back. She lay on the mattress and pretended that she was riding in an ambulance all the way to Atlanta.

Mrs. Eloise shunned a private room for a ward, so she could be in the exhilarating company of sick folks.

Her surgery was scheduled for the next morning, and Mrs. Eloise spent the evening discussing the finer points of hypochondria with a lady from Augusta who was in for her fourth round of exploratory surgery.

"Why, I been cut on so much that I look like a crossword puzzle, and they still ain't found out what's wrong with me," the lady said proudly.

"Well, I'm here for a complete hysterectomy," Mrs. Eloise announced.

The lady from Augusta peered at Mrs. Eloise with wistful eyes and tried to look as if she was in great pain.

Things started going wrong before daylight the next morning. When they came to get Mrs. Eloise to prepare her for surgery, in one of those typical hospital mix-ups, they wheeled her into the wrong area and a male nurse showed up with a razor in his hand.

"What you gonna do with that razor?"

"I'm gonna shave you."

"You're gonna shave me where?"

"Your pubis."

"My what?"

"Your pubis."

"What's that?"

"Your crotch, lady."

"You ain't shaving my poobuck, nor my crotch neither."

"Look, lady, I'm not used to shaving women either, but Dr. Titus said for me to come in here and shave the patient, and round here you don't give doctors any guff. Now, spread your legs."

"I most certainly will not."

"Look, lady, do you want to be operated on or not?"

"Don't you touch me. No man but my husband has ever seen my private parts."

"Well, the doctor's going to see your private parts when he operates on you."

"That's different. He's a doctor. He's used to such things."

"Well, I'm a nurse, and I've seen a few of those things in my life, too. Now, come on, lady, or I'm gonna catch hell," he said, reaching for the sheet.

"Don't you dare touch me, you prevert." Mrs. Eloise jumped up and slapped the male nurse across the face and took off out the door. She went flying down the hall with her hospital gown open down the back and her huge naked ass quivering like a bowl of jello.

She ran up to the nurses' station screaming bloody murder. The head nurse soon discovered the mistake, and they wheeled Mrs. Eloise into another area, where a female nurse shaved her poobuck.

After she had been shaved and scrubbed and painted with Merthiolate, they gave Mrs. Eloise a shot of morphine, and she floated into the twilight zone, imagining that she had a rare disease that Blanche Fletcher couldn't even pronounce the name of.

The operating room was cold, but Mrs. Eloise didn't mind. She was trying to remember where she was. The anesthesiologist placed the mask over her face and the lights went out.

When she woke up, she was still in a fog, but not too much of a fog to remember that she had just had a major operation. She immediately rang for the nurse.

"I need something for pain."

"What's the matter?"

"You know perfectly well what's the matter. I've just had a complete hysterectomy."

"No you haven't."

"What?"

Mrs. Eloise pulled up the sheet and the hospital gown, and to her dismay, there was not one stitch in her red-painted, hairless lower parts.

Mrs. Eloise felt like crying. "What happened? I was supposed to have my complete hysterectomy this morning."

"There'll be a doctor coming in soon to explain it to you."

In a few minutes, the doctor came in. "Good morning, Mrs. Conyers, how are you feeling?"

"About as well as can be expected without a complete hysterectomy."

"You don't need a complete hysterectomy."

"Don't tell me that. Dr. Morris said I needed a complete hysterectomy worse than anybody he'd ever seen."

"Dr. Morris is a sick man. He's been operating on people wholesale lately. He took out enough appendices and gallbladders to fill the room — all useless."

"But I need it! He said so! I need it bad!"

"Well, you almost had it. He even had the scalpel in his hand when the head doctor went into the operating room and suspended him from the staff. We've had five lawsuits filed against the hospital already."

"What kind of a doctor are you?"

"A surgeon."

"Well, how about you giving me my complete hysterectomy then?"

"Mrs. Conyers, for the last time, you don't need a complete hysterectomy."

It was all too much for Mrs. Eloise. So near and yet so far. She broke right down and cried.

What would she say to the Baptist Sunshine Auxiliary? How could she ever face them without a complete hysterectomy? She would be disgraced. Blanche Fletcher would never let her live it down.

The next day in the Atlanta paper, there was a front page story about the "mad doctor" who had been operating on everybody he could get to hold still long enough. He had been placed in psychiatric care, suffering from a mental disorder called greed.

The article also stated that a certain Mrs. Eloise Conyers had been "bravely lying on the table, while the mad doctor hovered above her, knife in hand, poised to remove healthy organs and change her life forever."

Mrs. Eloise sent Melvin out to buy twenty copies of the Atlanta paper.

As soon as she got home and made sure that everybody had heard the news about her "bravely lying on the table," she had a nervous breakdown. It didn't last too long, however. She was well enough to attend the weekly meeting of the Baptist Sunshine Auxiliary.

"I tell you, Gladys, I had the feeling when they put me to sleep that something was wrong. I had this strange feeling that I might not never wake up again."

There was no disputing the fact that Mrs. Eloise was a full-fledged celebrity. Her name was right there in the Atlanta paper, right in the middle of the biggest medical scandal of the decade.

Mrs. Eloise never did get her complete hysterectomy, but she did develop a case of bronchitis later on in life, which allowed her to hack and cough the rest of her days.

She finally passed on at the premature age of eighty-one from an inoperable case of natural causes.

Curtis Loach

I'M A MAN who has done a pretty good bit of traveling in his day. I been to New York City, and I been to Miami, Florida. I been to Charlotte and Richmond and Greensboro. I mean, I ain't just some feller you'd see on the street and say to yourself, "I bet that feller has traveled a lot." I ain't wearing no travel stickers on my forehead or nothing, but I was even in New Orleans, Louisiana, one time.

I also ain't trying to say that I know everything in the world they is to know, but I have been out of New Hanover County a couple of times. I guess what I'm trying to say is, of all the people I've seen (Oh! I went to Atlanta to a baseball game, too, a major league baseball game), in all them places I've been, I'd have to say that the downright damnedest man I ever did see was Curtis Loach.

He used to do and say the beatingest things of anybody in the world.

I mean, you take the time that his youngest son was born. Curtis claimed to be part Cherokee Indian. (I never did believe he was.) Anyway, Curtis said that he was gonna do like the Indians used to do and name his baby for the first thing he seen after the child was born.

Well, the first thing he seen was a can of paint, so he named the poor little boy Hi-Glo, Hi-Glo Loach. How would you like to drag that name around with you for the rest of your life?

And he was always telling jokes that he made up hisself. And they never were a damn bit funny.

He'd say something like, "Knock, knock."

"Who's there?"

"Alley."

"Alley who?"

"Alley Bamy," and then he'd bust out laughing like he was Bob Hope or something.

And if you was standing in front of him when he laughed, he'd spit all over you. He kinda gurgled and sounded like a commode flushing, with just about as much water. It was a downright disgusting habit.

I remember one time at a high school football game when the referee called back a touchdown that our boys had made, and our whole side of the field was up hollering. I mean, everybody in town was madder than hell. Well, that won't good enough for Mr. Curtis Loach. He was drunk as a fiddler's bitch, and he went running out on the field and called the referee a blind pissant. Then he picked up the football and let the air out of it with his pocketknife.

And I think one of the worst things that he done was he called everybody "Sweets": "How you doing, Sweets?" "Well, all right, Sweets." "I'll see you later, Sweets." It was aggravating as hell just to be around him.

Curtis never did own a car, but he had an old wore-out Ford tractor, and he'd drive that thing all over the place. He'd even drive it to town on Saturday.

Curtis lived in a mighty run-down old place about three miles out of town. It leaned to one side and he never did cut the grass in the yard. It used to get knee-deep in the summertime.

His wife used to have a baby every year. They must have had ten or eleven children. Their yard was always full of snotty-nosed kids running around and hollering and carrying on. If you drove up in the yard, they'd all jump right in your car and act like they was driving and go all through your glove compartment.

One time, Glen Gooden left the key in his pickup truck, and one of them little kids got it started up and run it right into the side of the house. Knocked part of the front porch down, and that's the way it stayed. And Glen had to spend a pocketful of his own money to get his truck fixed. Hell, he knew that there won't no use in trying to make Curtis and that hungry brood of his pay for it.

I remember that Curtis's old milk cow used to get out all the time and get into Mrs. Mildred Bennet's garden. Mr. Bennet told Curtis that the next time his cow got in Mrs. Mildred's garden, he was gonna pull all her upper teeth. Well, sure enough, the old cow got out again, and when Curtis went to pick her up, he looked in her mouth. Naturally, the cow didn't have no upper teeth. Curtis got mad as hell and was threatening to shoot Mr. Bennet, till somebody told him what any fool knows — cows don't have no upper teeth anyway.

He was a mess, but I'd have to say that Curtis Loach was also about the happiest feller I ever did see.

Well, one day a man showed up in town. He was real dressed up and talked with a yankee accent and was asking around about how to get to Curtis Loach's place. Nobody knew who he was or what he wanted, but we gave him the directions. It turned out that he was a big lawyer from Chicago, Illinois.

It seemed that Curtis's granddaddy had come from Oklahoma and had owned an old no-account piece of farmland out there, and damned if they hadn't found oil on the place. Curtis, being the next of kin, owned the place now. Just like that, Curtis Loach was as rich as all get out. I'm talking about filthy rich.

Now, here was an ignorant dirt farmer that never did have two nickels to rub together, and all of a sudden, overnight, he came into millions of dollars. I mean, the man gave him a check for $250,000 just for signing the papers.

Well, all hell busted aloose in our little part of the world.

The next morning Curtis went to town and bought him one of them big diesel tractors, and nobody was safe on the roads after that. He was roaring around town on that damn monstrosity, just generally terrorizing everybody, running up on the sidewalk and all. He run right into the light pole in front of the hardware store and knocked off half the electric power in town. He broke the light pole clean in two and didn't even slow down, just kept right on going.

When Sheriff Cox finally caught up with him and told him that he was gonna have to pay for that light pole, Curtis pulled out a wad of cash money big enough to choke a mule and peeled off a big handful of hundred dollar bills. He handed them over and said, "Ed, if that ain't enough, you know where to find me!"

Then he started buying things. He bought eight color televisions, three refrigerators, a washer and dryer, two living room suites (one for him and one for his wife), a haybailer, a thrashing machine, a corn picker, all kinds of discs and turn plows, fourteen shotguns, an electric stove with a self-cleaning oven, and he bought Simmon's Grocery Store slam out of popsicles. Damn if he didn't even buy a used bulldozer. He just went crazy.

Curtis Loach would buy just about anything that anybody would sell him. You couldn't even get close to his house for the salesmen. They were all over the place, coming from as far away as Virginia, selling everything from Cadillacs to sewing machines. Curtis and his family went through money like it was falling from the sky, but them oil wells in Oklahoma went on pumping and the money just kept on rolling in.

One day he decided he didn't like the music on the radio, so he bought the radio station to "put some decent music on the air." From sunup till sundown, all you could hear was Curtis's favorite songs. He liked bluegrass, and it was Bill Monroe and Flatt and Scruggs all day long.

His yard was full of swing sets, his fields were full of farm machinery, his pastures were full of prize cows, and his house was full of every kind of gadget you could imagine. He couldn't have squeezed another thing into that dilapidated old place with a shoehorn.

It was dangerous to even be around Curtis's neighborhood. His wife wrecked three brand-new Lincoln Continentals trying to learn how to drive. And she never did learn how. She finally just give up, and the three wrecked cars set out on the shoulder of the road in front of his house.

Charlie Daniels

Even with all the aggravation of Curtis driving all over the place in a super-charged diesel tractor, endangering life, limb and property, and in spite of all the mess that Curtis Loach's new-found wealth brought into our lives, I'll have to say that we done a damn good job of enduring it all. That is, we did until some fool sold Curtis Loach an airplane.

It was a single-engine job, and Curtis took about three hours worth of flying lessons, and then the skies over our part of the world became unsafe for birds. Imagine living in a town where a man who couldn't even drive a car would come flying an airplane over your house at 150 feet at twelve o'clock at night. It was nerve-wracking as hell.

I'll have to say one thing for Curtis, though. He looked after his family. He bought his wife a full-length white mink coat. It would have looked real good, but she dipped snuff and was always spitting down the front of it. After a while it looked like hell.

What all of us couldn't figure out was why somebody would buy one of everything in the world and live in a house where the rain fell right through the roof. But we didn't have to wonder long.

Curtis hauled off and built him a house like you wouldn't believe. It must have had thirty rooms. Everything was electrified. It had a swimming pool and a tennis court. (Curtis didn't know a damn thing about tennis.) It had three acres of the prettiest, greenest lawn you ever have seen. It was built out of fine stone with a paved, circular drive.

It had a reading room, sitting room, drawing room, den, dining room, blue room, living room, full basement, gymnasium, sauna, hot tub, solarium, library, gun room and a monstrous-sized kitchen. It was three stories of unadulterated fanciness, with six half-baths and eight full-baths, with enclosed shower stalls and king-sized sunken bathtubs. Now, for a family whose facility had been some thirty yards from the back door, and the biggest luxury there was the Sears and Roebuck catalog, that was a pretty fancy place to answer a call of nature.

The grounds had a greenhouse, a putting green, an archery range, guest house, eight-car garage, servants' quarters, and I forgot to mention the whirlpool alongside of the regular heated, chlorinated, olympic-sized swimming pool.

The paneling in the drawing room used to be in some Catholic church in Italy or somewhere, and a lot of the furniture was named after Looey something or other — some dead French king.

There was a dumbwaiter in the kitchen that served all the floors and an intercom system that would play music all over the house.

There was a chandelier in the living room that was bigger than a two-horse wagon wheel, with little diamondlike things just dripping off of it.

There was a burglar alarm, fire alarm, floodlights, riding stable and the gun room had a fireplace that was eight foot across and four and a half foot high, made out of native stone.

It was the fanciest, most uppity-looking, awesome, efficient, centrally heated and air-conditioned structure since the Taj Mahal.

Curtis had an announcement made over his radio station for everybody to come by and see it the day they moved in. Needless to say, all the women in town would have done anything short of killing to get a look inside Curtis's

Charlie Daniels

palace, and the men weren't a whole lot different, so damn near the whole town showed up that day.

It was like going to Disneyland. I mean, he had his own regulation-sized pool table and one of them televisions with the great big screen on it. It was a sight to see. That house was all, and I mean *all* that anybody talked about.

"Did you notice that Weatherby .300 magnum in the gun cabinet?" Or, "Gladys, she had a walk-in cooler, right in the kitchen, with sides of beef hanging in it." I mean, that's all you heard.

We didn't see much of Curtis in those days. Somebody said he was trying to learn how to play golf. After about six months, he showed up down at the pool room one night, right before closing time. He didn't try to tell no jokes and didn't even get on nobody's nerves. It was just, "Howdy, fellers," and he just sat at the bar and drank his beer.

Norman, I believe it was, said after a while, "How you liking the house, Curtis?"

"It's all right," Curtis mumbled.

"Did you watch the Cowboys' game on that big TV?"

"Naw."

"Somebody told me you had a horse up there that cost $100,000 dollars."

"Damn ole thoroughbred. Can't ride the son of a bitch."

"Curtis, Graham Fowler told me that you had ten full-time hands working up there."

"I can't understand a word that butler feller says, and if I get up to go to the bathroom at night, when I come back the damn sheets has been changed. And that woman that cooks can mess up a pot of beans worse than anybody I

84

ever seen."

I think that it dawned on everybody at about the same time, I know it did on me, that Curtis Loach was about the most miserable feller I ever did see. He took to spending his days going down to the old house and sitting on the porch. I seen him at the drugstore one day, and it seemed like he walked a little slower and his hair was a little grayer.

We was playing Clarkton one Friday night, and I mean it was an intense game. We scored right before the half, but that jackass in a zebra suit called interference on our boys and brought it back, so we went into halftime tied nothing to nothing.

Somebody said, "Remember that night that old Curtis Loach run out on the field and busted the football? Life ain't been the same around here since old Curtis got rich." We all agreed that maybe some of his jokes might even have been a little bit funny.

Did you ever have one of them déjà vu things happen to you? I mean, where you feel like you know everything that's gonna happen right down to the words people are gonna say? Well, one of them clicked in on me right about then. I heard it in my head before I heard it in my ears. A kind of a *waughhhhh* sound from a way off, and it kept getting louder and closer.

All of a sudden from out of the night and into the lights of the football field there came a big green diesel tractor. There's a cyclone fence at the north end zone, and he just ploughed right on through it.

There was cheerleaders and band players running, and Curtis Loach, as drunk as a fiddler's bitch, came driving onto the football field. He drove right out to the fifty-yard line and stopped. Damn if the crowd didn't give him a standing ovation, and then he rode around the field one time and drove away.

Boy! That crowd was so up and cheered so hard for our boys that we beat Clarkton thirty-one to nothing. It was a fine old night.

The next day it was in the Raleigh paper that the government was filing a multimillion-dollar tax fraud suit against Curtis Loach. It seems that Curtis had never filed an income tax return in his whole life. He just didn't know that you were supposed to. He started attracting attention when he started making all that money, but the IRS had never heard of him.

They audited and audited and figured and figured, and when they got done it turned out that all Curtis was gonna get to keep was his old farm, his new house and that diesel tractor he thought so much of.

They told him, "Mr. Loach, it looks like we're gonna have to take just about everything you've got."

They said old Curtis jumped up and laughed and said, "Come get it."

That big house they live in has changed a considerable amount. The grass in the yard is about knee-high. Almost all of the glass has been broke out of the greenhouse, and Curtis keeps a litter of bluetick hound puppies in the drawing room. The swimming pool is green and that bunch of little monsters have tore the dumbwaiter all to hell riding up and down in it. And the yard is full of snotty-nosed kids all running around and hollering and carrying on.

And I believe that Curtis Loach is the happiest feller I ever did see.

Chatham County

CHATHAM COUNTY HAD fell on hard, dry times. The merciless sun boiled down from a cloudless sky day after day, with no rain in sight. In fact, it hadn't rained in forty-five days.

The river didn't run anymore — it barely dribbled — and the smaller creeks and branches had given up the ghost long ago and become long, sandy-bottomed ditches. Even the leaves on the trees were withering, and the bright leaf tobacco, the very centerpiece of Chatham County economics, was burning up in the fields.

It was the summer of '56. Tempers were short and credit was shorter, and all in all a right miserable time for the unfortunates who made their livings toiling under the hot Carolina sun.

And, as if that wasn't enough, the good people of Chatham County got yet another kick in the head when they woke up on that hot July morning. Virgil Perkins had died during the night.

Virgil Perkins, high sheriff of the county for over twenty-five years.

Virgil Perkins, iron-handed segregationist, the man who had said that the whole United States government could go to hell along with that smart-ass yankee, Dwight David Eisenhower.

Virgil Perkins, who had single-handedly defied the highest court in the land and dared them to send one federal marshall into his county.

Virgil Perkins, champion of white supremacy, defender of Southern womanhood, deacon of the church, fixer of speeding tickets, who carried cases of store-bought whiskey in the trunk of his car at election time.

Virgil Perkins had passed away at the appallingly young age of seventy-nine.

It was 7:30 in the morning and the regulars were holding court at Moore's General Merchandise and Filling Station.

"It come over the radio at six o'clock this morning," Charlie Deaver said, lighting his fifteenth cigarette of the day. "They said that they didn't know when the funeral's gonna be yet."

"Ain't he got a boy out in Oregon?" Wade Poe asked of no one in particular. "It'll probably be two or three days before he can get home."

"Well, I'm gonna go whenever it is. Virgil was a damn good man and a friend to everybody in this county," Clarence Potter put his two-cents' worth in.

"Ain't no telling what's gonna happen around here now with old Virgil gone. The first thing you know they'll have the schools all mixed up, and it'll be the biggest mess you ever laid eyes on."

"Not if Garner Cheek gets put in office. He's the same

kind of man Virgil is, or was. He'll keep 'em in line."

"Baloney! Garner Cheek's balls ain't no bigger than English peas. He'll knuckle under the first time that bunch in Raleigh says 'boo.' "

"I'd like to see Buck Tally get it myself, if he won't in prison. He was the best damn deputy Virgil Perkins ever had, and I never did believe that he really shot that feller. Damn court just railroaded him, that's all."

"Well, it's a mess all right. Charlie, did they say anything about it raining on the radio?"

"Eighty-five degrees and clear. Hell, I believe it's forgot how to rain."

"You know, I seen Virgil day before yesterday, and he acted like he was feeling real good."

"You can't never tell about them heart attacks. Everette Tyson worked all day suckering tobacco and died at the supper table. Fell right over in a plate of beans."

"I reckon they'll bury him at the Bethel Church graveyard, won't they?"

"Well, surely they will, him being a deacon there and all."

"Well, look coming up the street. It's that son of a bitch from Connecticut. I reckon he's happy with old Virgil being dead and everything."

"I don't know why he don't just go on back up north where he belongs."

The door opened and in walked Robin Andrews — teacher, troublemaker, liberal, integrationist, yankee, educated fool and no-account bastard (as far as this bunch was concerned).

An icy silence fell on the loafers.

"Good morning, gentlemen, isn't it a beautiful day?"

Robin said, walking briskly into the store.

The only one who responded was Tommy the clerk. "Good morning, Mr. Andrews. Can I help you?"

"Yes, Tommy. I'll have two packets of unlined writing paper, please."

Tommy brought the paper to the counter and said, "Mr. Andrews, did you hear about Sheriff Perkins?"

"Yes, Tommy, I did. My aunt told me about it at breakfast this morning. It appears that Caesar is indeed dead. Thank you, Tommy. Put that on my bill, please. Good day, gentlemen." And with that, he walked out of the store and down the street.

"I'd like to bust his ass. I'd like to buy him for what he's worth and sell him for what he thinks he's worth. Tommy, I don't know why you even let that stuck-up jackass come in here for."

"You know damn well why I let him come in here, just like you know why you don't bust his ass. Mrs. Devereaux owns half of this county, and you know she wouldn't take kindly to anybody mistreating her favorite nephew."

"Well, that's the only reason. You know, old Virgil done his damnedest to get the school board to fire that prissy-acting son of a bitch, but no, they was all scared to on account of old lady Devereaux. That's the only thing that saves his ass around here."

"Who's Caesar?" Charlie Deaver wanted to know.

The atmosphere and the conversation was pretty much the same up the street at Mom's Cafe, except that the clientele wore short-sleeved white shirts and clip-on ties. These were the businessmen of the community, drinking coffee, smoking cigarettes and commiserating about things in general.

"Well, there's a good 'un gone," Paul Carter said. "Virgil Perkins was a hell of a man."

"Yeah, for sure. Who's in line for his job?"

"Garner Cheek's the chief deputy. Won't he get it?"

"Damn, I hope not. He'll get his ass up on his shoulders and be hell to deal with. He don't like me anyway."

"Hell, he don't like nobody."

"He ain't so bad."

"Well, he ain't all that damn good!"

"Boy, I wish old Buck Tally hadn't a-screwed up. He'd a-been the man for the job."

Virgil Perkins was laid out at Kinlaw's Funeral Home. Visitation was set for seven o'clock that evening, and almost everybody in town stopped by to pay their respects.

Remarks like, "He sure does look natural," and "Didn't they do a good job on him?" were heard over and over throughout the evening. And as the last of the mourners were filtering out into the muggy August night, it began to sprinkle rain.

The rain picked up and turned into a downpour, much to the delight of the residents of Chatham County. The thirsty ground greedily sucked up the rain for the first few hours, but as the night wore on and the ground saturated, the water began to stand in puddles and still it rained, as if nature was trying to make amends for the long dry summer.

The next morning the rain was still coming down, and the regulars at Moore's General Merchandise and Filling Station watched the water running through the street in small rivers.

"Did you hear anybody say when they're gonna have Virgil's funeral?" Wade Poe asked.

"Tomorrow morning at ten o'clock."

"Who's gonna do the honors?"

"Reverend Buchanan and some preacher they're bringing in from Siler City. They say that every judge in the county's coming, and some of that bunch out of Raleigh. I reckon they want to make sure Virgil's really dead."

"That's just like them damn politicians, to crowd up the church so there won't be room for all the people around here to get in. Everybody's planning on going."

"Did the boy from Oregon get in?"

"They tell me he ain't coming. Sent a telegram."

"Well, if that don't beat all. You mean to tell me that he ain't coming to his daddy's funeral?"

"That ain't no way to do at all."

"Well, you know him and Virgil never did get along after he came back from college."

"Well, that don't make no difference. He at least ought to come home and bury his daddy."

"Damn, I'm glad to see this rain."

It rained all night and was still raining the morning of the funeral. The river was swollen and red clay mud of Chatham County was a quagmire, knee-deep in places.

The dignitaries arrived; the pallbearers donned their white carnations and dressed in their Sunday finest. The little community descended en masse on Bethel Baptist Church. The hearse got stuck in the mud driving into the churchyard, delaying the funeral for forty-five minutes while Fletcher Barnhill went home to get his tractor and pull it out. The church was full to overflowing, and about a hundred people stood outside in the rain, a testimony to the popularity of Virgil Perkins.

The casket was open for viewing, and the family

(including the prodigal from Oregon) were seated. Reverend Buchanan was standing in the pulpit wearing his best funeral face. The choir, under the direction of Brother Ben Phillips, looked prim and proper in their freshly starched robes, and Pauline Suggs was seated behind the big pipe organ playing softly. Flowers lined the front of the church and Reverend Buchanan cleared his throat.

"Dearly beloved," he began, "we are here to mourn the passing of a great man, a pillar of the church and a source of strength and pride to this community. The choir will now sing one of his favorite hymns, 'Shall We Gather at the River.' "

Brother Ben Phillips moved his hands in an upward motion, and the choir rose as one. "Shall we gather at the river, the beautiful, the beautiful river," they sang in the properly subdued fashion befitting a funeral. When the choir finished and sat down, Pauline Suggs flipped a page of her music and played ever so softly as the preacher from Siler City stood up and told about what an enormous loss the community, the county, the state, the country and the whole world, for that matter, had suffered.

"He was a man among men, a paragon of virtuous works, a loving father, a faithful friend, a conscientious civil servant who had faithfully served his fellow man for over a quarter of a century."

When he finally finished, the choir went into "Softly and Tenderly," and then Reverend Buchanan stood up to deliver his eulogy as Pauline Suggs's organ whispered in the background.

Pauline was the local piano teacher — a chubby old maid, who wore thick horn-rimmed glasses. She had had a secret crush on Brother Ben Phillips for years and had even

93

had erotic dreams about him. Pauline always played well, but she played her very best when Brother Ben was directing the choir. She could sight-read the most difficult of pieces with nary a hitch, but Pauline could not hardly play a note without music.

She loved playing the church songs, and it gave her a weekly chance to advertise her talent, but her first love (besides her secret passion for Brother Ben Phillips) was show tunes and the works of W. C. Handy and Jelly Roll Morton.

The service had been arranged so that when Reverend Buchanan finished his eulogy, Pauline would go into "Rock of Ages," and the pallbearers would come forward, take up the casket, and carry it the short distance to the graveside.

But as Reverend Buchanan was rapidly finishing up, Pauline Suggs suddenly realized that she did not have the music to "Rock of Ages." She panicked. She tried to get Brother Ben's attention, but he was listening intently to what the good reverend was saying.

"Brother Ben," she whispered. "Brother Ben." She just couldn't get his attention. She was a nervous wreck.

"And he will be sorely missed," Reverend Buchanan's resonant voice proclaimed. This was Pauline's cue to start playing "Rock of Ages." But how could she play when she didn't have the music?

Thirty seconds passed and nothing happened.

"And he will be sorely missed," Reverend Buchanan thundered. Still nothing.

Brother Ben Phillips slipped discreetly out of his seat and eased over to Pauline. "Play, Pauline," he whispered.

"I can't. I haven't got the music."

"And he will be sorely missed," Reverend Buchanan boomed for the third time.

"Play, Pauline. Play something." Brother Ben's whisper was getting louder.

"I can't. I don't have the music. You know I can't play without the music," and Pauline burst into tears.

"Play, you fat cow. You're screwing up everything," said Brother Ben.

Pauline was bawling audibly by now, and in desperation she launched into the only song she knew by ear, a rousing version of "The St. Louis Blues." The volume from the big pipe organ was deafening, and Pauline Suggs, tears streaming down her face, was banging on that organ like the phantom of the opera.

Confusion reigned supreme. One of the pallbearers stood up, and then the others, thinking that it was time to retrieve the casket, stood up and started toward the front of the church.

Marvin Kinlaw, the undertaker, who was in the vestibule when the ruckus started, tried desperately to reach the pallbearers before they got to the casket, but in his haste he slipped and sprained his ankle. He yelled, "The lid's not closed. The lid's not closed, you fools." But the organ completely drowned him out.

The pallbearers picked up the casket and proceeded out the door of the church. You could see the deceased's head bobbing around as they went down the steps.

The congregation rose and followed.

As the pallbearers made their way to the graveside, one of them on the right side of the casket slipped in the mud, and the domino theory went into effect as all three pallbearers on the right side fell to the ground, dropping their side of the casket.

The good people of Chatham County watched in horror as the mortal remains of Virgil Perkins slipped out of the casket and kerplopped onto the ground.

"Look, Mama. He ain't got no pants on."

And it was true. Old Virgil was as naked as a jaybird from the waist down.

If confusion reigned supreme before, it was an absolute monarch now. Children were crying, men were hollering and women were fainting. And above it all, "The St. Louis Blues" thundered out of the open church door.

People were running around like crazy, but nobody seemed to know what to do. From the stricken crowd stepped a figure, none other than Mr. Robin Andrews, the no-good son of a bitch from Connecticut. He threw his raincoat over Virgil's exposed parts and, with the help of the dazed pallbearers, managed to get Virgil off the ground, back into the casket, and closed the lid.

The soggy pallbearers then continued to the graveside as if nothing had happened. Reverend Buchanan was in shock, but he somehow managed to finish the service. "Ashes to ashes and dust to dust," and it was all over.

Everybody just wanted to go home, and they rushed away as soon as the last "Amen" was said. Brother Ben Phillips finally got Pauline to stop playing the organ, and she came out of the church door a broken woman. Brother Ben took her home in his car.

Reverend Buchanan called Robin Andrews aside. "That was a fine thing you did, my boy, taking charge in the midst of chaos. I know that Brother Virgil would want me to convey his gratitude to you if he were able. What a terrible thing to have happen to such a fine man, don't you think?"

Robin Andrews glanced sideways at the good reverend and said, "I came to bury Caesar, not to praise him." And then he walked off across the churchyard, spattering Carolina mud on his Connecticut shoes.

Trudy

DON'T GET ME wrong. Trudy had her good points. Why, that woman could be so sweet she could charm a bee into her mouth. But when she got on an ornery binge, it was "Katie, bar the door!"

It was when she was in one of her latter moods one day when we got into a real donnybrook, something about me staying out all night and coming home a little on the tipsy side. I mean, we went at it. We started off hollering at one another and ended up with bare knuckles and frying pans. That is, she ended up with bare knuckles and frying pans.

I'll tell you how I am. I never could bring myself to hit a woman. Pushing and shoving and holding her is kind of all right, but no hitting. Of all the things my daddy had drilled into my head, that was one I always remembered.

"Only sissies hit women," he used to say, and I can't ever remember a time in my life when I wanted to be a sissy.

Anyway, it was nitty-gritty time in our kitchen, and she

was coming toward me with one of them big cast-iron skillets when I just said, "The hell with it," and walked (well, really kinda run) out of the house.

Now, I can't see no harm in a man taking a little drink now and then, and if he stays out late with the boys once in a while, that ain't no reason for a woman to get her nose out of joint. I mean, it wasn't like I went out and got knee-walking every night in the week, and the more I thought about it, the more aggravated I got at Trudy. Just who in the hell did she think she was, anyway?

That night about six o'clock, after Trudy had left for her job (she tends bar at the Red Horse Saloon—now there's one hell of a fine beer joint, but that's another story), I sneaked into the house and packed some clothes, picked up seventy-five dollars that Trudy thought she had hid from me, and lit out to the Greyhound Bus Station, where I bought me a one-way ticket on the midnight express to Houston, Texas.

That's where everybody from our part of the country went when they left home.

"What you gonna do when you graduate?"

"Goin' to Houston."

"How about you?"

"Goin' to Houston." Everybody and his brown dog wanted to go to Houston.

The truth of it was, if you was willing to work your ass off, you could get a job in Houston making fairly decent wages.

Now, I didn't leave Lafayette half-cocked. No sir, my best friend lived in Houston. Old Joe Ed Tibideaux. Hell, Joe Ed was big-time in Houston, Texas. He had a fancy apartment in a big, high-rise building and was making all grades of money and running with all manner of pretty, young nymphomaniacs, according to his letters. I tried to call Joe Ed before I left, but there was no answer. I figured he was out to some major party or something, so I bought me a half-pint of Jim Beam and smiled all the way to Texas.

I hate like smoke to say it, but I was a little bit disappointed in Joe Ed's lifestyle. His high-rise apartment was on the second floor of building 26B at Sagebrush Apartments in Pasadena, Texas, and the only female I ever saw at the door was a tired-looking little lady with the Jehovah's Witnessess.

Hell, he didn't even have a job and ended up borrowing half of the thirty-six dollars I had left.

I was so confounded disappointed that I felt like turning around and going back to Louisiana, but I thought about that big, black frying pan and decided I'd better stick it out in Houston for a while.

Now, I might have my idle spells, but I always been a man that believes in working. So early the next morning I was anwering ads in the *Houston Post* newspaper, and I'll have you know that I got me a job making $8.75 an hour, plus overtime, starting the next day.

I don't know if anybody ever told you or not, but it's hot as hell in Houston, Texas. I mean from the time the sun goes up till she goes down, it's murdersome hot.

But let me tell you something else you might not know. It's the same way in Lafayette, Louisiana, and us old boys from over that way can handle it pretty well. They love us coon-asses in Houston, Texas.

I done real well up till the first payday, and then I really messed up. I mean, I threw away three hundred dollars doing things that I don't even remember, and all I got out of it was one monumental hangover.

The hangover's what really done it. I was so sick that in a weak moment, while I was hugging the plumbing, I swore that I wouldn't take another drink for six months. Now, I may say something and not mean it, like swearing, and not do it worth a flip, but if I sure enough swear, I'll be damned if I don't believe that going back on it will bring a feller the worst kind of luck.

Well, when I woke up about two o'clock that afternoon, the first thing I wanted was a beer, and I got one, too, and had it opened and was fixing to take a swig when I remembered my oath. I was just barely able to pour that nice cold beer down the drain. So there I was, stuck in Pasadena, Texas, and couldn't take a drink for six months. Hell, there ain't nothing else to do in Pasadena, Texas.

Anyway, I took to staying around the apartment most nights and watching Monday Night Football and getting downright disgusted. I was sitting around one night when I got this wild, crossways hair, and I sent old Trudy a postcard. It just said, "I'm sorry," and gave the return address.

About three weeks later, I got one back from her that said, "You ought to be."

The next day I got up the courage to call her, but the phone at the Red Horse Saloon was out of order, so I finally reached her at home about three o'clock in the morning. The conversation went something like this:

"Hello."

"Trudy?"

"Yeah."

"It's me."

"I know."

"Did you get my card?"

"Uh-huh."

"I quit drinking."

"I'll bet."

"No, really."

"I'll bet."

"Can I call you again?"

"Maybe."

"I sure do miss you."

Silence.

"Trudy?"

"Yeah."

"I said, I sure do miss you."

Silence.

"I'll call you again real soon."

"Bye." And she hangs up the phone.

Now, I'm not trying to make out like that phone call was a sterling reconciliation, but hell, it was a start.

I called her a few more times and got pretty much the same results, but she finally got to where she was about half-civil on the phone and admitted that she missed me just the tiniest little bit.

Well, that was good enough for me. I was off and running and making Ma Bell real happy burning up the telephone lines, telling Trudy how I was a changed man, and how I thought that we ought to get together again. Now, she didn't think too much of that idea to start with, but after a while I guess she must have got to feeling sorry for me and she said we'd give it one more shot.

Now, I was just about ready to jump clean through the roof, and I really wanted to leave that night, but with all my other bad habits, I never was one to leave a man in a bind, so I figured on giving a two-week notice on my job.

Well, I worked out my notice, and I was mightily anxious, but happy, and then on a Friday afternoon I was all done. I drew my pay and, along with what I'd saved watching Monday Night Football, I had a right handsome sum. So I called and reserved me a seat on an airplane at 7:55 the next morning.

I was all packed and fixing to go to bed when Joe Ed walked in and said that a man was giving him three hundred dollars to drive his car to Dallas, and that he'd give me half of it to go along and help him drive.

The last thing that I wanted to do was detour through Dallas, Texas, but old Joe Ed was my best friend, and that $150 wouldn't hurt nothing. So I said, "What the hell," and put my suitcase in the trunk and took the first turn driving.

The truth is that I ended up driving the whole way, and when we got to Dallas, it was just about midnight. Joe Ed gave me directions to a place called the Backstreet Social Club.

This feller came out of the bar and took the car, and me and Joe Ed went inside where this dude in a black tuxedo gave Joe Ed some money and offered to buy us a drink. Joe Ed took him up right off, but me, in remembering my solemn pledge, realized that I still had two days to go.

I should have walked out right that single solitary minute. I should have bit my tongue when I heard it saying, "Oh, what the hell, it's just two more days. Let me have a shot of Crown straight with a little bit of Seven-Up on the side."

I was gonna have that one drink and get up off the

barstool and light out for Lafayette, Lousiana, as fast as I could, when this blonde-headed girl sat right down next to me.

Now, I hadn't been within touching distance of a woman in six months, and she smelled real good. Even then I most likely would have been all right if she just hadn't smiled, and I mean right at me.

I should have chewed my tongue half in two when I heard it say, "Can I buy you a drink? Make that two."

I don't know what happened to the next two hours, but the next thing I knew we were playing slot machines in this back room, and every time I'd take a drink, she'd get prettier.

I had lost about thirty-five dollars on the slot machines, and my blonde-headed friend was starting to look a lot like Farrah Fawcett when the dude in the tuxedo comes up and asks me if I'd like to play some seven-card stud. Now, I ain't meaning to brag, but I play a pretty mean game of seven-card stud poker.

I won the first two hands straight out and was $110 richer. Then I lost a couple of hands, and then my hot streak started. I mean, I couldn't lose. I was betting and raising and dragging in them poker chips,and just generally raising hell. "Ante up. Give me another drink. Drag 'em in." I had a pile of chips in front of me that reached halfway up to my chin when this big tall feller walked up to the table and the game just stopped.

He was the fanciest dressed man I ever did see. I mean, he had on a three-piece silk suit with a big gold watch chain across his belly. He had a thick black handlebar moustache and fancy alligator shoes.

"Good evening, gentlemen." His voice sounded like

the bass singer in the Oak Ridge Boys. "Mind if I join you?"

"Why sure, Mr. Walker."

"Certainly, Mr. Walker."

You'd a-thought he was the Pope the way they all acted around him.

He came right up to the table and sat down and started laying hundred dollar bills on the felt. And when it came time for his deal, I declare I never did see a man handle a deck of cards like that. He could fan them all out on the table and turn one card over, and flip the whole damn deck over. I mean, he was good.

Things went along for about an hour with him winning and me doing a right fair job of holding my own. Then all of a sudden there was a big pile of chips in the middle of the table, and everybody had dropped out except for yours truly and old John Lee Walker. We had five cards apiece on the table, and I had a pair of queens showing and another in the hole. I was feeling real good about it, so I bet, and he raised, and I raised again. The very next card he caught a king and I caught that other snuff dipper. Hot damn! Four queens! Bet, raise, raise. I knew I had him, so when the last card fell, I bet a pile. I never expected him to raise, but he did, and healthy, too. I figured him to be trying to buy me out, so I raised him real strong. I'll be dogged if he didn't raise me back, and before it was over, every cent I had was in that pot.

He asked me what I was so proud of, and I laughed and turned over my other two queens and reached for the pot.

"Don't touch the money." His voice literally made the glasses rattle, and then he turned over his three hole cards and every damn one of them were cowboys. Four kings! I was so disappointed at seeing all that money being pulled away from me that I guess I just lost my head. "You're a cheating son of a bitch," I hollered.

The whole room stopped dead still. I mean, you coulda heard a germ sneeze. He got so red in the face I thought he was going to explode, but he said (really kinda calm, considering the size of his voice and all), "Boy, I'm gonna give you just five seconds to retract that statement. A man in my profession can't afford to be called a cheat."

I don't know what in the world makes a coon-ass so stubborn after he's had a few drinks, but I just stood there and tried my best to look like John Wayne. That is, I stood there until I saw his hand go inside his jacket. I figured he was reaching in there for something besides his fountain pen, and I done been shot one time and guns make me nervous, so I jerked up one of the empty chairs and brought it down across his big head. I thought he was gonna get up, so I popped it to him again and took off running.

Do you know that big rascal, after being hit in the head twice, still pulled out a Smith & Wesson snub-nosed .38 and started popping off rounds in my direction? I was turning over tables and thinking that at any time I was gonna look down and see blood coming out of a hole in me.

Now, I'll have to admit that John Lee Walker was one hell of a poker player, but he was the worst shot I ever did see. Out of six bullets the only thing he managed to hit was a bottle of Old Granddad behind the bar, and I was heading through the front door to the wide open spaces.

Well, when I went out the door, I took a hard left and ran

right into the smallest cop on the Dallas police force. I knocked him winding and was moving off down the sidewalk like the Orange Blossom Special when I was tackled from behind by a policeman considerably bigger than the first one. I took a swing at him but he ducked and brought his billy club down on my kneecap. Well, then I did land a punch. I mean, I cold-cocked him. By that time, I was swimming in a sea of blue, and I punched and kicked at everything that moved. But then they had my arms, my legs and my head, I just couldn't move no more.

Eight of 'em. It took eight of Dallas's finest to get me under control, and one little dried-up old night judge to slap a $2,500 fine on me and have me carted away to the drunk tank.

Boy, when I woke up the next morning, there ain't no way to tell you how I felt. I was hung over something awful and sore in every muscle, and when I remembered what I had done last night, I just laid back down on the floor and went back to sleep.

Sometime later the guard came and kicked me awake and said that somebody had paid my fine and I could go.

I had clean forgot about old Joe Ed Tibideaux, but there he stood big as life and grinning. I couldn't wait to get outside and find out how Joe Ed had got ahold of all that money.

It's kind of a long story, but to make it short, when all the shooting started the night before, Joe Ed took refuge under the poker table, which in the course of events got turned over, spilling money to the four winds and a goodly portion into Joe Ed's pockets. He sneaked out the back while half of the DPD was wrestling with me and went to a big hotel and spent the night. Being good enough to remember me when he woke up at two o'clock that afternoon.

Joe Ed said that since he'd come out so fat, and seeing as how a big part of that money had been mine anyway, that if I'd promise never to tell anybody, he'd split it with me. And once he'd deducted the $2,500 for the fine, I had just enough left for a beer, a bus ticket and a dime for the telephone.

I called collect and Trudy refused the charges the first three times. When she finally accepted the call, she said, "Now, just what in the hell is Mr. Changed Man doing in Dallas, Texas? You were supposed to be here at 9:30 this morning!"

"You wouldn't believe it, Baby. There was this freak thunderstorm and our plane got grounded in Dallas, and this feller in the men's room stole all my money at gun-point, and I got beat up, and my face is bruised and my clothes are torn and I'll be in on the Greyhound bus at 9:15 tonight."

"I got a funny feeling that you're lying. Have you been drinking?"

"Baby, I told you I quit drinking."

"You better not be lying to me."

"Baby, would I lie to you?"

Silence.

"Will you pick me up at the bus station?"

"Maybe."

Yes sir, that Trudy is one tough woman.

The Story Of Uneasy Rider

HOWDY! MY NAME is Robert E. Lee Grant, and I hail from Bluefield, West Virginia. I'm one of nine children, the youngest in fact, and they're a conservative bunch, to say the least. So in 1972, when I turned eighteen and grew my hair down to my shoulders, you wouldn't believe the grief I took from my family.

Why, you would have thought that I had single-handedly started the Second World War, or that, at the very least, I was a depraved child molester. My own blood and bones called me hippie freak, radical rebel and all manner of endearing names, and they even hinted that I might be of questionable gender.

Well, I took all of their verbal abuse right handily, I'd have to say, but when my brother, Harold, came home drunk late one night, roused me out of a deep sleep, and tried to scalp me with a dull Buck knife, I said this is just too much.

I guess that's what got me thinking about going to

Charlie Daniels

California. From what I'd seen on television and read in *Rolling Stone* and other enlightening publications, the people in California all kept their hair long, smoked wacky tobaccy, wore sandals and did pretty much as they damn well pleased.

Why, California was just chock-full of spiritual freedom and free love, and besides, the Jefferson Airplane and the Grateful Dead all lived out there.

Now, I'd been working at Mr. Finklestein's hardware store in the afternoons and on weekends since two days before my twelfth birthday, and being a thrifty person, I'd saved most of the money I'd made except what I'd spent on my passion.

My passion was a '56 Chevy with headers, a racing cam, tachometer, hot mufflers, thirty-six coats of black paint and a peace sign painted on the hood in gold metal flake. Oh, it was the hottest, most uppity-looking car you ever laid eyes on, and it could outdrag anything on wheels in Bluefield, West Virginia.

Anyway, when I told my family that I'd decided to go to California, you'd have thought I was taking a one-way trip to Sodom or Gomorrah. My mama near fainted and cried and carried on about how my feet had strayed off the slippery path of righteousness. She moaned all about the house, wondering where she had failed in raising me.

My oldest sister, Joyce, who wore her hair in a bun and was married to the fire-and-brimstone preacher who was pastor of the All Faiths Free Will Non-Denominational Church, had her husband, Brother Bob Bledsoe, come and talk to me.

Well, he didn't really talk. He more like kinda hollered, and you'd a-thought he was preaching to a whole congregation of perverts and hard of hearing, hell-bound sinners. I'll have to admit that Brother Bob did shake me up some.

He told me what a satanical place California was, and how everybody out there had turned their backs on all the decent things in the world and were living in sin, and how the whole state was going to break off and sink into the Pacific Ocean.

He was really working up a full head of steam, and I don't remember how Moses and the children of Israel got into the picture, but he was stomping around the living room, waving his arms in the air, sweating like a mule, and just generally running in high gear.

When he got to the part about what an abomination my long hair was, he had to stop and take a breath. That's when I jumped in and said that as near as I knew from all the pictures I'd seen, Moses and the children of Israel hadn't never been near a barber shop.

Well, Brother Bob just lost it. His face turned the color of a fire engine, his voice went up fifty decibels, and I was downright afraid that he was going to have a stroke.

He called me a black sheep and a curse on my family's good name. He said that I was a lost cause and was doomed to wander the earth in sackcloth and ashes, and that I might as well go on out to California and drown with the rest of the sorry, sinful whoremongers and homosexuals with long hair and beads, and imbibe strong drink and waller in dope and incest, and that at least I wouldn't be spreading the serpent's venom in Bluefield, West Virginia.

Anyway, Brother Bob made California sound like such a fun place that even though I had decided to leave in two weeks, I just couldn't wait to be on my way. So I gathered

113

Charlie Daniels

up my blue jeans, put on my tee shirt that said KEEP ON
TRUCKING on the front, and lit out.

I had money in my pocket, a stash in the glove compartment, and the radio turned up real loud. I was riding high
and flying low, and that old Chevy was cooking down the
mountain and holding to the curves like a champ. I was on
my way to California.

Anyway, late that evening, I was tooling south out of
Memphis on Route 51 with an illegal buzz and the speak-
ers rattling on the radio when I heard a low hum, and I
could tell that my left rear tire was going flat.

I pulled over on the shoulder of the road, opened the
doors so I could still hear the radio, and unlocked the trunk
to get the jack and the spare. Well, I just damn well
couldn't believe it — that old spare tire was as flat as a
flitter. I couldn't do a blessed thing but just ease that old
Chevy down the shoulder at about five miles an hour.

Just as the flat tire was getting plum down to the rim, lo
and behold I came to the outskirts of Jackson, Mississippi.
But the only thing close to the highway was this little bar
and grill sort of a place called the Dew Drop Inn.

I barely made it to the parking lot, and when I got a
closer look at that old Dew Drop Inn (it had beer cans all
over the parking lot and a sign in the window that said
AMERICA, LOVE IT OR LEAVE IT) I figured that I'd
better clean up my act.

I reached in the back seat and got my ditty-bop hat —
one of them leather deals with a roach clip on the hatband
— stuffed all my curly locks up under it and made a
beeline for the door.

It was pretty dark inside, and I was sure glad to find out
that there wasn't nobody there but the bartender, and he

was watching a rerun of "I Love Lucy" on the television. I kind of sidled up to the bar and said, "Excuse me," but just then Ricky Ricardo said something funny, and the bartender, who looked about two sizes larger than Roosevelt Grier, laughed out loud, and it sounded like thunder.

When he finished laughing, I said, "Excuse me," again, and he turned his watermelon-sized head toward me. When he saw me for the first time, the expression on his face was like he'd just smelled something real bad. I said, "Uh . . . could you please, sir, change a dollar for me so I could use your pay phone, please, sir?"

He never said a word. He just opened the cash register and slapped three quarters, two dimes and a nickel on the bar, picked up my dollar and turned back to the television set in time to see Lucy spill a bowl of spaghetti all over Fred Mertz's new suit.

I groped my way back to the phone booth, looked in the book under Road Service, and got the number for Ray's 24-Hour Shell Station and Emergency Road Repairs. I got ahold of Ray on the first ring, told him my problem, and old Ray said for me to wait right there, that he was on his way.

Well, I didn't bother to tell him that I'd just about as soon be in Moscow, but that I sure as hell couldn't go anywhere else.

When I got back to the bar, Lucy and Ethel were having one whale of an argument, and Man Mountain Dean was just short of rolling on the floor. I waited until a commercial came on, and said, "Please, sir, could I please have a beer?"

He looked at me like I'd just invited him to a rattlesnake convention and slapped a can of Jax and a glass on the counter. Then he turned back to the TV, which suited me just fine. I took my beer and moved down to the very last barstool in the dark, content to wait out old Ray in total oblivion.

After I'd been sitting there for about ten minutes, the front door swung open and in walks this dude in hog-washer overalls, brogan shoes, and a Funk's Hybrid Seed baseball cap.

He stomped up to the bar and said, "Hey, Jimmy, you old dog. How's your hammer hanging? Draw me a tall, cool one."

Well, he got his beer and walked back to the jukebox, where he played "Okie From Muskogee," and every time the chorus came up, him and the bartender would sing off-key with Merle Haggard.

Me, I just sat clear back as far as I could get in the dark and hoped that old Ray would get there in a hurry.

Everything was going along pretty good, and Merle Haggard and Hogwashers and the bartender were just finishing up "The Fighting Side of Me," when Hog-washers said kind of like an afterthought, "Hey, Jimmy, whose fancy machine is that in the parking lot with them mag wheels and four on the floor and that big peace sign painted on the hood?"

Well, Jimmy didn't say nothing. He just jerked his thumb in my direction. Hogwashers leaned back on his barstool, peered through the dark, and when he saw me, a big mean-looking grin came on his face. He said, "I didn't know that they was having a gay liberation get-together in Jackson. I mean, complete with fancy automobiles with the footprint of the American chicken painted on the hood. Well, do tell, what's Mississippi coming to?"

116

I knew right then that there wasn't no percentage in my staying, so I pulled out a dollar, laid it on the bar, and headed real quiet and respectful toward the door.

Now, Jimmy and Hogwashers was laughing, but at least they weren't moving, and that pleased me to no end.

It looked like I was gonna make it to the door in one piece, but just as I was abreast of the coin-operated pool table, the door slammed back and in walked some people I really didn't want to see.

There was six of them in all: a big man with a white sidewall haircut and arms about the size of my head; a tall, skinny beanpole feller; a fat dude with his belly hanging over a pair of dirty Bermuda shorts; a sour-looking gray-headed man in a cowboy hat; a real dumb-looking sort of a dumpy feller with a big mouth, and when he grinned his two front teeth were as green as a gourd; and a lady . . . well, maybe *lady* wouldn't be the right word — more like a middle-aged, frowsy-looking old chick with cantaloupe-sized tits and a mini skirt two sizes too small, and you could see varicose veins on her wrinkled legs. She had a real high beehive hairdo that kept falling down on the sides and the reddest lipstick I ever did see, smeared all over her mouth. I mean, she was a real honey.

They were in a high old mood and drunk as all get out, and they hadn't noticed me, which I was real glad about.

I was detouring around by the cigarette machine on my way to the exit when the dude with the bucket-sized arms started toward the bar and ran right into me, knocking me into Miss Varicose Veins. She almost fell on the floor — just barely being saved by a combined last-ditch effort by Beanpole and Cowboy Hat.

I got my hands on the doorknob and was fixing to

skedaddle when I felt a big paw on my shoulder jerking me around. "Hey, boy, just who in the hell do you think you are?" It was Bucket Arms. "Running into a lady like that and not even apologizing!"

"Yeah, just who in the hell do you think you are, boy?" Beanpole joined in. I guess he wasn't smart enough to think of something original.

I looked at Varicose Veins and said in my nicest, most politest voice, "I'm awful sorry, ma'am. Please forgive me for being so awkward and clumsy." Beehive looked at me with her bloodshot eyes, and I felt so low that I could have jumped off a brick and committed suicide.

"You can't forgive a dog after he's done bit," she said in a voice that sounded like a cross between a high-pitched frog and a Chihuahua howling.

I tried again. "Well, I hope you can find it in your heart to overlook my stupidity." But they just weren't buying.

"Didn't your mama ever teach you to take off your hat when you're talking to a lady?" said Bucket Arms. Without thinking, I reached up and grabbed the crown of my ditty-bop hat, and when it came off, my curly locks fell all the way to my shoulders.

They all started laughing, fit to be tied, and Beanpole hollered, "Well, excuse us, ma'am. We didn't know you was a little girl. Just excuse us all to hell."

My ticker almost jumped track, and I just knew that my time had come as they started walking around me, looking at me from all angles, and calling me names that I always thought were reserved for people like Adolf Hitler.

Old Green Teeth had not opened his king-sized mouth except to grin, and when he did speak it was kind of unintelligible and sounded something like "Sombitch,

sombitch, looka queer, sombitch, Missipi, hotdamn, sombitch."

Well, now I ain't no shrinking violet; I been in plenty of knucklebusters back in Bluefield, West Virginia, but I knew I didn't have a chance with this bunch.

Bucket Arms laid his baseball glove hand on my shoulder and said, "You know what I think I'll do? I think I'll just stomp a mudhole in your pansy ass and walk it dry." I was scared as hell and desperate. I don't know what made me do it, but right about that time, I just hauled off and kicked old Green Teeth on the kneecap as hard as I could.

He screamed like the whistle on a steam-powered coal train, which kind of seemed to shock everybody for a few seconds, and right about then I came up with the most brilliant idea of my entire life.

"You're him," I hollered. "You're the one!" I jumped back and grabbed a chair from one of the tables and held it above my head. Before they had time to clear their whiskey-muddled minds, I shouted, "Watch him, boys, he's real tricky. He's the one that the FBI sent down here to spy on the Ku Klux Klan."

I was moving a little too fast for them to catch up, and I sure intended to keep it that way.

"My laig's broke! My laig's broke!" old Green Teeth was yelling, which kind of added to the confusion, and I moved on quickly, really laying it on thick and heavy.

"This man has been going around tearing Wallace stickers off the bumpers of cars." That kinda got to them for a couple of seconds, and seeing as how there was no turning back now, I waded on in. "He hangs out with all them long-haired hippie-type homosexuals. He's probably even got a Commie flag hanging up in his garage. This man is a snake in the grass. He's a blight on the face of America and Mississippi."

They all looked kind of stunned, and I rolled on. "He may look real dumb, but don't let him fool you. He wants to do away with the Constitution, the Golden Rule, and the American way of life. He wants to tear down the Stars and Stripes and put up the Hammer and Sickle."

They all turned and looked at their green-toothed buddy, which fit perfect into my plans, and I started easin' toward the door cause I knew that the spellbinding wouldn't last but a few seconds.

Old Green Teeth evidently was getting some feeling back in his leg, and when he saw them looking at him in such a strange way, he started saying, "Now, wait just a damn minute. You've all been knowing me all my life. Why, I'm a dues-paying member of the John Birch Society, and I belong to the Antioch Baptist Church, and I don't even own a garage. You can call and ask my wife."

I guess he had some more to say, but I didn't hear it. I pushed open the door and lit a shuck across the parking lot.

I could have just kissed old Ray. While I was inside going through my shenanigans, old Ray had been oustide fixing my flat tire and was taking my car down off the jack when I came running up. I jerked out a twenty dollar bill, threw it at him, and jumped in on the driver's side.

Boy, that engine sure did sound sweet when I cranked her up, and I could see in the rear view mirror that the whole Dew Drop Inn was emptying into the parking lot. I shoved her into first gear and dug out for the highway, but I guess about that time my mean streak must have come into play, cause I just couldn't resist the temptation of chasing them around the parking lot a little bit.

I'll swear, I never did see a bunch of drunks move so fast — that is, all but old Green Teeth, and he was limping pretty bad.

They were doing pretty good staying out of the way of the hottest Chevy ever to come out of Bluefield, West Virginia, except for the doll in the beehive. She fell down on the first pass, and her mini skirt flew up over her waist. She had the ugliest pair of legs I ever did see.

They were all huffing and puffing and looking behind them. That's how Cowboy Hat and Beanpole ran full tilt right into the side of the Dew Drop Inn. I saw the bartender come running up to the side of the car with a baseball bat in his hand, so I spun her to the left, and I'll be damned if he didn't climb the pole that held up the Miller High Life sign. I never did see a big man move so fast.

Yeah, it was all good fun, but I figured I'd better split before somebody got the bright idea of calling the cops.

I was in third gear when I hit the shoulder of the road, and I showered that old Dew Drop Inn with loose gravel one more time. I was doing ninety-five miles an hour when I hit high gear, and I didn't let off very much till I was almost to the Arkansas line.

I cruised on for a while, but I figured out the traveling life just wasn't for me. So I just took a right in Omaha, and Bluefield, West Virginia, you sure look good to me.

Mrs. Effie

MRS EFFIE McPHERSON was a good Christian woman. She had raised five sons and five daughters to manhood and womanhood.

Mr. Efrem McPherson passed away not long after the last child had left home, and Mrs. Effie came into a considerable amount of money, by our county's standards, on account of Mr. Efrem's insurance policy.

Well, a new television station had just come on the air in Greensboro, bringing television to our part of rural North Carolina for the first time. And Mrs. Effie McPherson was the first one in the county to have a television aerial on top of her house.

Mrs. Effie hadn't never seen a television before in her whole life, and to tell the truth, she didn't even know what it was. It had been her children's idea. They thought that since she would be spending so much time alone, the television set would be a good source of company for her.

The day they brought it out to hook it up, it being the

first television in the county and all, quite of few of us had stopped by to get our first look at "the radio with pictures on it."

They got it hooked up and turned it on, and Mrs. Effie went running out of the room. A few minutes later she came back in, all dressed up in her Sunday best.

Roscoe, her youngest son said, "Mama, what did you go get all dressed up for?"

"I don't want them people seeing me in that old house dress."

"What people, Mama?"

"The people on that thing," Mrs. Effie said, pointing at the television set.

"Mama, them people can't see you."

"Why, sure they can. I can see them. And if I can see them, they can see me."

"Mama, I'm telling you, them people can't see you."

But no amount of persuading could convince Mrs. Effie that the people on television couldn't see her. So she sat down on the couch, pocketbook on her lap, and started her first day of television watching.

Well, everything went pretty good until the first commercial came on. It was a soap commercial, and the feller doing it said something to the effect that Tide was the very best laundry soap you could buy.

Mrs. Effie hopped up and said, "Well, I declare, I been using Rinso for thirty years. I thought it was the best you could get. Roscoe, I want you to go to town tomorrow and get me some of that other stuff."

Mrs. Effie turned into what was probably the most avid television watcher in history. She watched it from the time they signed on in the morning till they signed off about twelve o'clock at night.

She watched the soap operas, and talked about the characters as if they were personal friends of hers: "Sarah, I tell you, my heart just went out to Elizabeth when she found out that John was gonna have to have that operation. And then that Paula. You know, I just don't trust her. Anyway Paula told Elizabeth about J.J. and Martha getting married, and that upset the poor thing even more. Then, as if that won't enough, Judge Higgins — you know, he's Elizabeth's mama's second husband — he called up and said that Elizabeth's mama was drinking again, and I don't know what all. I tell you, Sarah, them poor people have more trouble in their lives. I feel so sorry for them."

She watched the baseball games, the football games, the Friday night fights, the situation comedies, the variety shows, the news, the weather forecast, the "Today Show," the "Tonight Show," the sermonette and all the commercials.

Roscoe claimed that she even watched the test pattern sometimes.

If Mrs. Effie saw anything advertised on television, as far as she was concerned, it was the best. She bought soap, cake mix, soda pop, ice cream, chewing gum, bleach, flour, meal, breakfast cereal, canned goods, baking powder and even sent away for a course in judo.

And she shared her new wisdom. "Roscoe," she said one day, "you ought to get you a Chevrolet automobile. Dinah Shore was just saying Sunday night how good they was."

She watched Walter Cronkite's news broadcast religiously. She was always quoting him, but she couldn't quite handle his name. "Walter Crockett was saying last

125

night that President Eisenhower is gonna have to get tough with them Russians."

She used to get awful upset about people getting murdered on the detective shows. When justice was finally done, she'd sit there and clap her hands and laugh, "You see there. I knew they was gonna catch you. You can't get away with something like that. I tried to tell you before you shot that poor feller, but no, you wouldn't listen to me, would you? I told you, didn't I? It serves you right!"

Somewhere along about that time the television station put on Saturday afternoon wrestling.

A lot of other people had television sets by that time, and wrestling was a big favorite with everybody. But Mrs. Effie went absolutely crazy over it.

The old woman would get so excited that she'd be jumping up and down hollering, "That's right! Bust his liver out! Do him like he done you while ago! Yeah! Smack him again!"

And Mrs. Effie had her favorite wrestlers and her unfavorite wrestlers. Her very favorite wrestler in the whole world was Bobby Joe Bobbitt, "The Texas Tornado." She idolized him. He was always one of the good guys. He was an all-American looking sort of a feller and just radiated fair play and decency.

He had a mystery hold that he used to put on his opponents that he called his "West Texas Brain Scrambler." It would freeze the other feller's head, so he'd be looking right straight up.

And Bobby Joe was the only one that could put the feller's head back right. The bad wrestler would follow Bobby Joe around the ring, beseeching him to fix his head back.

After a while, out of the goodness of his heart, Bobby Joe would do it.

If the Texas Tornado was Mrs. Effie's favorite, her most unfavorite was the Raging Russian. Mrs. Effie probably came closer to hating the Raging Russian than she did anybody else on the whole planet Earth.

He was a great big, ugly feller. He had a coal black beard and a bald head, and he was about the meanest looking hombre you ever did see. And he used to do awful things to his opponents. He'd rake their eyes across the ropes or stomp on them when they were down.

One Saturday afternoon Bobby Joe Bobbitt and Greased Lightning had a tag team match against the Boston Bruiser and the Crazy Cajun.

Well, sir, about halfway through the match, who comes out but the Raging Russian. He crawls right into the ring, sneaks up behind the Texas Tornado and hits him right in the back of the head, knocking him out cold.

Mrs. Effie was about to have a heart attack. That Russian devil was messing with her boy.

They got the Raging Russian on camera. He had to speak through an interpreter, cause he didn't speak no American at all.

The announcer asked the Raging Russian how come he had got in the ring and knocked Bobby Joe Bobbitt out.

The interpreter turned around to the Raging Russian and babbled something. "He says that he doesn't like the Texas Tornado because he's a coward, and that every time he sees him, he's going to knock him silly."

Mrs. Effie was so mad that her head was almost smoking.

About that time, the Texas Tornado come running up

and was gonna put it on the Raging Russian, but a whole bunch of fellers grabbed both of them, and they just stood there hollering at one another.

Bobby Joe started hollering that he demanded satisfaction, and the Raging Russian said that he'd fight the Texas Tornado any place, any time.

Bobby Joe upped and said, "Well, what about next Friday night at Triad Arena at eight o'clock, and the ticket prices will be three and four dollars."

The Raging Russian said that would suit him just fine, that he'd be there.

Then the Raging Russian said something directly to Bobby Joe, and Bobby Joe asked the interpreter what it was.

The interpreter said, "He says that he will grind your weak American body into the canvas."

Now, that really pissed Bobby Joe off, and he tried to get aloose and go after the Raging Russian.

"You dirty Communist, next Friday night I'm gonna break your neck!"

If it hadn't a-been for them fellers holding them, they'd a-went at it right there.

The announcer jumped in and said, "You heard it right here, folks! Next Friday night at Triad Arena, a grudge match between the Texas Tornado and the Raging Russian! Ticket prices three and four dollars. Plan to be there now!" And then Saturday afternoon wrestling went off.

Mrs. Effie got right on the telephone to Roscoe.

"Roscoe, did you see what that old Raging Russian done to Bobby Joe this evening?"

"No, Mama, I didn't."

"Well, he snuck right up there in the ring with Bobby

Joe and popped him right in the back of the head, and Bobby Joe won't even looking. Knocked him out. Did you ever hear of such a lowdown thing in your whole life?"

"No, Mama, I didn't."

"But they're gonna fight up at Greensboro next Friday night, and Bobby Joe's gonna whip him good. I hope he breaks his old Russian neck."

Roscoe got to thinking. Mrs. Effie's sixty-eighth birthday was coming up next week. What better present to give her than to take her up to Greensboro to see her boy beat the hell out of that Russian? It was only sixty miles.

Roscoe got busy and got Mrs. Effie ringside seats.

That's all Mrs. Effie talked about that whole week. "Going up to Greensboro Friday night to see Bobby Joe beat the stuffing out of that old Russian with the bald head."

The Greensboro paper had a big ad that week saying that it was the fight of the decade, an American hero was defending the honor of this great nation against a Russian.

Well, Friday night rolled around and Mrs. Effie was so excited that she couldn't hardly contain herself. Me and Edna and Roscoe and Thelma is good friends, so Roscoe got us tickets, too, and asked us to ride up with them.

Triad Arena was packed to the rafters, and Mrs. Effie McPherson was on the very first row.

When they started the preliminary bout, Mrs. Effie turned to her son and said, "Roscoe, where's Bobby Joe?"

"He'll be here after a while, Mama. These other two fellers is gonna wrestle first."

"Well, how do you suppose he'll get here?"

"In a car I reckon, Mama."

"Do you think he'll be pretty mad when he gets here?"

"I guess he will, Mama."

"Which corner is he gonna be in?"

"I don't know, Mama."

"Well, I hope he's over here by us."

The preliminary bout was pretty good that night, but Mrs. Effie hardly knew it was going on. She was waiting for her idol.

After the preliminary bout, Triad Arena started buzzing with excitement, and Mrs. Effie was buzzing right along with it.

The time had finally arrived. A spotlight swung over by this entrance and in come the Raging Russian. He had on a red robe with "The World's Greatest Wrestler, The Raging Russian" printed across the back of it in big letters.

He had a whole bunch of policemen escorting him, and he kept growling at the crowd. Everybody booed at the top of their lungs, and people threw popcorn boxes and such at him.

Then they started playing "The Star-Spangled Banner" on the public address system and everybody stood up. The spotlight swung around again, and out walked the Texas Tornado in a red, white and blue robe, and you'd a-thought the roof was gonna cave in. I ain't never heard such a noise in my whole life. It took the referee a good ten minutes to get the crowd quieted down enough to introduce the wrestlers.

"And in this corner, weighing two hundred and forty pounds, from Central Siberia, the Raging Russian!"

Everybody booed for five minutes. The Raging Russian didn't care. He strutted around the ring with his hands up over his head like he'd already won.

"And in this corner, weighing two hundred and ten

pounds, the pride of Denton, Texas, USA, Bobby Joe Bobbitt, the Texas Tornado!"

The place just went absolutely crazy again.

It was to be the best two out of three falls, and the Texas Tornado started out like a house on fire. He had the first fall won in just a few minutes.

Mrs. Effie was ecstatic. "I knew he'd do it, I just knew he would. Bust his liver out, Bobby Joe!"

Then the Raging Russian came out smoking, pulled some dirty tricks and won the second fall.

It was down to one fall.

The Raging Russian come out smoking again. He bounced Bobby Joe all over the ring, and it looked like Bobby Joe was done for. He was staggering around the ring, about to fall down, and the Raging Russian grabbed him and threw him down on the canvas.

This won't going at all like Mrs. Effie planned it. "Get up, Bobby Joe, you got to get up!"

Somehow or 'nother, the Texas Tornado managed to get up and started beating the stuffing out of the Raging Russian. Triad Arena was about to fall down.

But just as Bobby Joe was about to apply his famous head hold, the Raging Russian stomped him on the toes. Bobby Joe grabbed his foot, and the Raging Russian popped him right in the face with his elbow.

"Why, you dirty son of a bitch!" Mrs. Effie yelled.

"Mama! What did you say?" Roscoe asked.

But Mrs. Effie didn't hear him. She was up heading for the ring, and for a sixty-eight-year-old woman, she was right agile. She climbed into the ring before anybody could stop her and started beating the Raging Russian in the head with her pocketbook.

131

The crowd loved it. Everybody was on their feet cheering Mrs. Effie on.

She was really socking the Raging Russian with that pocketbook, and he was yelling, "Somebody get this crazy woman off of me!"

Mrs. Effie was astonished. "Why, you old faker, you ain't supposed to speak no American!" And she flailed away again with that pocketbook.

Two policemen started into the ring after Mrs. Effie, but several of the crowd grabbed them and held them back. It was turning into a riot.

The Raging Russian was running around the ring with his hands over his head, trying to stay away from Mrs. Effie's lethal purse.

Mrs. Effie was a terror. While she swung the purse with her right hand, she reached out with her left hand, and grabbed ahold of the Raging Russian's beard, and it came off in her hand. The crowd went beserk.

Several more policemen went running up into the ring and finally got things settled down while two of them tried to hold a kicking, biting Mrs. Effie McPherson.

After the policemen had established order of a sort, the two policemen holding Mrs. Effie started leading her out of the ring. The crowd booed real loud. They didn't want to see Mrs. Effie go to jail.

Out of the noise and confusion stepped none other than the Texas Tornado, Bobby Joe Bobbitt. He said something to the two policemen, and they turned aloose of Mrs. Effie. Bobby Joe put his arm around her and raised her hand in the manner of a champion and walked her around the ring, while the crowd thundered and they played "The Star-Spangled Banner" again.

Oh, it was a grand old night. Everybody went home happy, except the Raging Russian.

Mrs. Effie was a celebrity. Her and the Texas Tornado signed autographs and posed for pictures for an hour and a half.

On the way home, Mrs. Effie was talking sixty miles an hour. "Did you see him, Roscoe? Did you see him put his arm around me?"

"Yes, Mama, I seen him."

"Did you see him kiss me right on the cheek, Thelma?"

"Yes, ma'am, Mrs. Effie."

"He sure is a fine boy, ain't he Roscoe?"

"Yes, Mama, he sure is a fine boy."

The next day, on the sports page of the Greensboro paper, there was a half-page picture of Mrs. Effie, standing there with the Raging Russian's big black beard in her hand.

That night on the seven o'clock television news they had Mrs. Effie beating on the Raging Russian with her purse. When Mrs. Effie saw herself on television, she almost passed out, and it was all anybody talked about for two weeks.

I saw Mrs. Effie at the grocery store a couple of days later and she was describing the action to Mrs. Ethel Shaw. "Ethel, I seen that Bobby Joe was done for and that dirty rascal was gonna whip him, sure as the world. So I went up there to help Bobby Joe out. And do you know that lying Russian can speak American? I don't believe he's even a Russian. Why, Ethel, he even had a false beard! I never seen such a faker in my whole life."

After Mrs. Effie got through describing her adventure in Greensboro, Mrs. Ethel said, "Effie, why don't you come

Charlie Daniels

by the house this evening? Grace and Gladys are coming by, and we're gonna make some peach ice cream."

"I can't Ethel, I got to get home and see how John's operation come out. You know J. J. and Martha has split up already and they ain't been married but two weeks. It's about to drive poor Elizabeth crazy, and Paula's going around telling everybody that Elizabeth told around that she was gonna leave John after he got out of the hospital, which as you know is an out-and-out lie. You know John and Elizabeth love one another. I never did trust that Paula. I'd like to pull her hair out."

And you know something? I believe she would.

Swami Swafford

TO SAY THAT Farley Swafford was ugly would be like saying that the Atlantic Ocean was a mud puddle. Or like saying that the Mississippi River was a drainage ditch, and that the Pope was a Freewill Baptist.

Farley radiated ugly.

His eyes were real close together, and his hair looked like broomstraw and always stuck out from under his cap. His nose was about the size of an Irish potato and he had buck teeth. People used to say that Farley Swafford could gnaw an ear of corn right through a picket fence.

His voice sounded like a cross between a mad bull alligator and the whistle on a midnight train. He talked louder than any man I ever did see, and every other word was a cuss word.

You couldn't believe a damn word that Farley said, either. He'd rather climb a tree and tell a lie than stand on the ground and tell the truth.

I remember one time he said that he seen an angel sitting

up in a tree back in the woods. He said that the angel told him he was looking for Clyde Holliday to tell him to quit drinking, because his days were numbered.

Poor old Clyde got so scared that he quit drinking, joined the Smith's Chapel Methodist Church, and ain't backslid to this day.

Another time Farley claimed that he had struck oil out on his place. "I was out in the field siding corn," he said, "and the plow point struck a rock, and sploosh, here the son of a bitch come, right up out of the damn ground, roaring like a damn steam engine."

"What did you do, Farley?" somebody asked him.

"I stuck the rock back in the hole and stopped the son of a bitch up," Farley answered.

"Why did you do that?"

"The confounded thing was scaring the hell out of my mule. He tore down a half an acre of corn before I could get the poor son of a bitch calmed down."

Farley believed in ghosts, and to hear him tell it, he seen them all the time.

"I was coming by the cemetery last night about twelve o'clock, when I seen this white thing floating around over the headstones. Well, I got out of the truck and walked up to it, and the damn thing disappeared. Just gone, disappeared, just like that," he said, snapping his fingers.

We all knew it was a lie, cause you couldn't pay Farley Swafford to go within a mile of a graveyard at night.

Farley also claimed that he could see into the future, that he knew what was gonna happen before it happened.

"Buck, your wife is gonna have twins, one boy and one girl," Farley would say, trying to look real mystical like. Funny thing is, Buck's wife won't even pregnant. But

Farley didn't care. He acted like everybody believed every word he said.

Every time somebody would tell him something that had just happened, he'd say, "I seen it, I seen it in my sleep last night. I knew that was gonna happen."

A few years ago, a whole bunch of hippies come in here from California and bought the old Benson farm next to Farley's. They sure were a strange-looking bunch. The men all had real long hair and beards, and the girls all wore real long dresses and went barefooted. And the whole bunch — men, women and little babies — was all living in one house. They called it a commune.

They said that they was gonna raise their own food and live off the land and commune with nature.

Well, they bought a mule and a bunch of plows and hoes and stuff and lit into farming. The only trouble was that most of them hippies was city folks and knew about as much about farming as a hog knows about an airplane.

Farley took to hanging around over there with them, telling them that he could see into the future and that they were gonna have a mighty poor crop that year. Well, hell, any fool could see that.

Now, of all the things that Farley Swafford claimed to know, there was one thing in the world that he really did know: Farley was a hell of a good farmer.

Them hippies almost starved to death that winter. I mean, they just barely made it through till spring. The next year at planting time, Farley showed them how to plant and fertilize and weed, and them hippies made a bumper crop.

They all thought that Farley Swafford had hung the moon or something, showing them how to make that crop and all. They got to thinking that he was some kind of a wise man or something, and they believed every word that he said.

Now, that suited Farley just fine, and he played the role to the hilt. They all took to calling him Brother Sunshine.

Somewhere along about that time, they got Farley to smoking that stuff that they all smoked, and Brother Sunshine started having visions. Farley also let his old stringy hair grow down to his shoulders and grew a full beard.

Well, Brother Sunshine had a vision one night that it was gonna be one fierce winter. He said it was gonna snow a lot and that everything was gonna freeze up, and that all them hippies had better get their asses busy gathering up wood if they didn't want to freeze to death.

They all got mighty busy, and they sawed and chopped till they had a pile of wood you wouldn't believe.

The twenty-seventh of December, it started snowing. It snowed for two days and the temperature dropped down below zero and stayed that way. It broke every record that the weather bureau had. I mean, it was flat out miserable. But all them hippies was snug and warm, and old Farley added another feather to his cap.

Farley soon took to wearing a long, flowing, white robe and beads around his neck, and he carried a long stick that he called his staff. He was the damnedest looking thing that you ever seen in your life.

He'd be standing out in the middle of a field with all that old long hair blowing in the wind, with all them hippies gathered around him, spouting off about brotherhood and claiming that he knew everything in the world.

Well, Brother Sunshine had another major league vision. He said that the roof of the courthouse was gonna cave in.

Now, our courthouse was real old and hadn't been particularly well took care of. People had been saying that it was gonna fall down for thirty years, but when we heard what Farley had said, we all laughed fit to be tied. It got to be the biggest joke in the county.

I couldn't begin to tell you how it happened, but one night about eleven o'clock the roof of the courthouse just collapsed and fell smack in. Everybody got to wondering if old Farley really was having visions.

After that, Farley just slap quit farming or doing anything else for that matter, except for sitting around, smoking them funny-looking cigarettes, and telling them hippies about the visions he had. And they believed him, too. They done anything he told them to. He coulda told them to go stick their heads in a fire, and they'd a-done it.

Then Brother Sunshine got on a roll. He predicted the death of Lacy Collins's milk cow, a flood in Sampson County, a corn blight in Indiana, an earthquake in Japan, an uprising in North Africa, and a plane crash in Ceylon. Brother Sunshine was going international. This was getting ridiculous. I mean, here was Farley Swafford, a loud-mouthed, ugly-as-hell dirt farmer, and he was turning into some kind of a Moses or something.

It got to where everybody in town was going out to the commune to talk to Farley.

"Farley, do you think I ought to leave my old lady?"

"Farley, am I gonna get that piece of land I'm bidding on?"

"Farley, who's gonna win the Super Bowl?"

It got to where you had to stand in line to talk to Farley Swafford.

Them hippies made him a big chair like a throne and

built a shelter over it, up on top of this high hill, and Farley would sit up there all day long, smoking that stuff and dispensing wisdom.

It got to where people from out of state were coming around to see Farley, or, as he preferred to be called in those days, "Brother Hadj Abdoul Rama Sunshine."

Some TV people out of Raleigh come to see Farley, and he predicted right on television that they was gonna strike oil in Mexico. Well, I guess you all know what happened. They sure enough did find oil in Mexico, and the lines out at Farley's place got longer and longer.

We was getting used to all the publicity, but when I seen Farley's picture on the cover of *People* magazine, I damn near fainted.

I mean, it was all like a dream.

One day this dark-skinned feller come to town wearing a purple turban. He was real polite, kept bowing and scraping, and he asked us how to get out to Brother Hadj Abdoul Rama Sunshine's place.

It turned out that this feller was from India, and he had come to see if Farley could go over to India and have a get-together with this other bunch of fellers that was in the same line of non-work as him.

Farley was gonna go, too, till he found out that he was gonna have to get on an airplane. Farley said that there won't no way that he was gonna get his feet off the ground.

Anyway, they finally worked it out that some of them fellers would come over here and see Farley.

Well, sir, you should have seen them fellers that come from India. There was this one feller that was kinda the leader. I mean, he was all sported out in this sort of a white gown, and his hair was white and it hung down all around his head, and he had a white beard that hung down below his bellybutton. He was carrying a big flower, and he laughed all the time.

There was six other fellers dressed like him, except that their gowns were orange and they were bald-headed. I mean bald-headed. Not a hair or a whisker anywhere. They were a sight.

They came to town in three great big, long, Cadillac automobiles. But they insisted on walking the three miles out to see Brother Hadj Abdoul Rama Sunshine. Don't ask me why they walked when they coulda rode in them fancy automobiles, I don't know. But they was a peculiar bunch anyway.

Some of us decided that we'd better go along and make sure that they didn't get run over by a load of pulpwood, so we jumped in Jeter's car and kinda drove slow. Them fellers did walk single file all the way out to Farley's.

When they got there, them hippies strowed flowers from the road all the way up to where Farley was sitting in his big chair, smoking one of them water pipes.

"Come in, brothers," Farley said, and he sounded like he was trying to talk like a yankee. "Welcome."

Them fellers all bowed and sat right down on the ground and crossed their legs. Everybody got real quiet, and you could hear the water bubbling in Farley's pipe.

Finally the one that hadn't never been to a barber spoke up and said, "Brother, we come in peace and admiration. We have come from far across the great ocean, where we heard of your great wisdom. We are humble men and much indebted to you for consenting to receive us."

"Well, that's all right," Farley said in his yankee voice. "What can I do for you?"

"Brother, we come lo this great distance in search of knowledge and enlightenment. We seek the answer to a question which has perplexed us and our kind for many centuries."

"Well, let's have at her," Brother Hadj Abdoul Rama Sunshine said, slipping back into his Farley Swafford voice.

"Thank you, Brother," the little flower-toter said, and then them bald-headed fellers started doing some kind of a chant. I mean, they went on for thirty minutes, and when they finally shut up, the little feller said, "We are much in your debt and we pay you homage for consenting to consider our humble inquiry."

"Well, ask the son of a bitch."

"Yes, Brother. The question is — What is the meaning of life?"

Things got so quiet that you could have heard a worm cough, and Farley took a big hit off of that water pipe and said, "The meaning of life is to live."

Them fellers all just sat there in deep thought for a while, and then them bald-headed fellers started babbling at one another, and then they all stopped and the little feller said, "We are much enlightened, Brother. Please accept our most humble gratitude. Peace on you."

"You're welcome, and piss on you, too," Farley said.

Then them fellers walked back to town, got in them Cadillacs, drove to Atlanta, got on a plane and flew all the way back to India.

I mean, them fellers come all that way just to spend one hour with Farley Swafford.

Oh, I could tell you a whole lot more about things that happened, like the movie stars that come to get Farley's advice or the bunch of people that wanted Farley to run for president.

The best-looking woman I ever seen in my life tried to get Farley to go back to California and move in with her, and when Farley said no, she broke down and cried like a baby and threatened to kill herself and carried on.

And then one time this holy roller preacher come to town and accused Farley of being the devil. Well, that made Farley Swafford mad. He said that he hated the devil worse than anything in the world, and he predicted that something bad was gonna happen to the preacher. Sure enough, the next day the preacher got slapped with a paternity suit by a sixteen-year-old girl's parents, jumped bail, and ain't never been heard from since.

Well, we got word one day that Farley said that he'd figured out how to make hisself invisible, and that he was gonna do it because he couldn't get no rest, what with people always bothering him.

Nobody really believed that Farley could make hisself invisible, but one day not too long after that some of them hippies showed up in town wanting to know if we'd seen Brother Sunshine.

Well, we hadn't seen him, and we ain't seen him till this day. Farley Swafford just disappeared. I mean, right into thin air — white robe, staff and all.

There's been a lot of speculation about what happened to Farley. A lot of people think he just plain run away. Lawson Beal swears that he seen him on the street in Fayetteville one day. Somebody else said that he'd decided to move in with that good-looking woman from California. Somebody even said that they seen a strange light in the sky the night he disappeared, and they figured that he'd been picked up by a spaceship.

Now, I don't claim to have any idea what happened to him, and I wish you wouldn't tell nobody that I told you this, cause they'll accuse me of being crazy. I'll admit that I'd probably had too much to drink. But I was on my way home and damn if my car didn't run out of gas right at the graveyard. It was late at night, and I ain't no superstitious man, but I didn't like being right there by the graveyard, so I decided that I'd just lock the doors and sit in the car till somebody come along.

I seen it out of the corner of my eye at first. It was this white thing floating just above the headstones. I don't need to tell you I was mortified. I was so scared that I thought I was gonna die. I got out of that car and I ran till I fell down on the ground, and then I got up and I ran some more.

The next day the sun was shining but I still kind of shivered when I went back to pick up my car. But things look different in the daytime. So I walked over to the graveyard where I'd seen the white thing.

The only thing that was there was a long stick stuck up in the ground with a white piece of cloth hung up on it.

I wouldn't a-thought nothing about it, but when I took the piece of cloth down, it turned out to be a long white robe, and I could a-swore I heard somebody say in a loud voice, "Leave the son of a bitch alone."

Christmas At The Line Shack

THE SNOW FLIES early in the high country. The north winds whip down out of Canada and the temperature plunges to forty below, and them high plains become a vast white wasteland.

Waiting out the winter in a line shack is boring and tedious, but somebody's got to do it. Somebody's got to see after the cattle in the wintertime, but why in the hell did it have to be me? And even if it did have to be me, why in the hell did I have to be stuck all winter with Shorty Pollard?

Now, it ain't that I got anything against old Shorty. It's just that I'm a man who loves to talk — they say back at headquarters that I'd carry on a conversation with a fencepost. Well, I might as well have had a fencepost for company as far as Shorty was concerned. If he said three words a day, it was a strain on him.

Don't get me wrong. Old Shorty was as fine a hand as a man could ask for. He could ride and rope with the best of

145

'em, and that fool could cook like nobody's business, and he listened real good. In fact, I guess Shorty Pollard was just about the best listener I ever did see. But when it came to answering back, a "yep" or a "nope" was about all you ever got out of him.

Nobody knew much about Shorty. He drifted in one day from somewhere down in Arizona, and I think that asking for a job was about the longest sentence anybody ever heard him say.

So here we were, with three months left on the winter and me just dying to carry on a conversation with somebody, and him acting like he was deaf and dumb.

Now, Mr. Rawlings (he owns the ranch) frowns on drinking when you're on company property. In fact, he downright forbids it, except at Christmas time. You could get as drunk as Cooder Brown at Christmas time, as long as you was sobered up by the twenty-sixth of December. Now, me being the kind of feller that likes to do what's right, I never would take a drink on the ranch anytime except Christmas time, and this year wasn't gonna be no exception. I'd brought three bottles of good Tennessee sourmash whiskey up to the line shack with me, and I was just waiting for Christmas.

I got in the habit of marking off the days on the calendar, cause a man can lose all track of time when he's holed up in the high country for four months.

One morning after we got up, I said, "Shorty, did you realize that tomorrow is Christmas Eve?"

"Nope."

"Well, I've got something special for Christmas, Shorty," and I reached under my bunk and pulled out one of the bottles. "Will you be having a drink with me tomorrow?"

"Reckon."

Damn, he made me mad. You offer to share the only whiskey in fifty miles with a feller, and all he'll say is "Reckon." But I didn't say anything, cause like I said, old Shorty was a fairly decent sort.

Christmas Eve morning arrived gray and windy, and it was snowing pretty good.

"Shorty, I'll tell you what. I'll ride out by myself this morning if you'll stay around here and cook us up something special. Is that all right with you?"

"Yep."

I went out and saddled up. It was cold as blue blazes as I rode up the draw checking on the cows, and I was real glad to get back to the line shack. The first thing I did was uncork one of them bottles.

Meanwhile, Shorty had outdone himself. I mean, he had it smelling real good in there. He'd cooked up a pot of his tasty stew with dumplings, and he had biscuits and two apple pies baked.

"Well, here's looking at you, Shorty," I said and turned the bottle up and knocked off a whopping snort of that sourmash whiskey. I passed the bottle to him and he did the same thing.

We ate our vittles, and after that we made pretty short work of that first bottle.

Now, Shorty didn't know about them other two bottles, so when I brought another one out from under my bunk, he actually smiled.

I was getting loose as a goose and feeling downright sociable. "Shorty, that's damn good whiskey, ain't it?"

"Yep."

We was pretty well into that second bottle, and I was talking my head off, but as usual Shorty wasn't having nothing to say. So I just shut up after a while and we both just sat there drinking.

It was a little after dark when we uncorked that third bottle, and by that time we was both pretty drunk. I guess I was even getting silly. I started singing Christmas carols, or at least what I could remember of them, and I kept mixing them up, like, "Silent night, midnight clear, hark the herald, we three kings, sleep in heavenly peace."

I guess it was getting on around eleven o'clock when the miracle happened. Shorty Pollard said something. His tongue was getting pretty thick and I couldn't understand him, but he really said something.

"What'd you say, Shorty?" I asked in shock.

"Et tu, Brute?" Shorty said.

"Shorty, what in the hell you talking about?"

"To be or not to be," Shorty said, his voice rising.

"Shorty, you're not making a damn bit of sense."

"What light through yonder window breaks?"

"Shorty, it's dark outside, and it ain't but eleven o'clock. They ain't no light breaking by yonder window."

"Be gone, thou cream-faced loon."

"Shorty," I said, "I don't give a damn if you are drunk. I ain't gonna let you talk to me like that." And I stood up. Well, at least I *tried* to stand up.

"At least we'll die with harness on our backs," Shorty hollered.

"You ain't putting no harness on me, and we ain't gonna die. We're just drunk. And if you don't stop insulting me, I'm gonna smack you upside the head with a stick of stovewood. You're talking crazy."

"Canst thou not minister to a mind diseased, pluck from the memory a rooted sorrow?" He must have went on for five minutes. Then he jumped up on the table and I barely caught the bottle before it hit the floor.

I was getting mad. "Shorty," I said, "if you had a-busted that bottle, I'd a-whipped you like a forty-dollar mule."

But Shorty wasn't paying no attention to me. He was off and running, ranting and raving.

"Oh, oh, oh, all the perfume in Arabia would not sweeten this little hand."

I thought he'd just gone loco. "Shorty," I said, "I think you'd better go to bed. You need some sleep."

"Sleep!" Shorty shouted, "Macbeth doth murder sleep!" He jumped down off the table and ran over to the fireplace and picked up the poker. "Charge, men!"

I thought for sure he was gonna hit me with that poker, and I got up and ran out the door as fast as I could, under the circumstances. It must have been about thirty below zero outside, and the wind was blowing something fierce. I went out to the shed and picked up an old horse blanket and snuck back up and peeped in the window. Shorty was sitting on the floor still babbling. After a while he fell back on the floor and I figured he'd passed out, so I went back inside and drug him over to his bunk and put him on it.

Shorty mumbled in his sleep all night long, but he never did say anything that made any sense.

The next morning, the sun was shining and it was one fine Christmas Day.

When I woke up, my head felt about the size of a pumpkin, and my mouth was dry and I just generally felt like a dead dog.

149

Charlie Daniels

Shorty was stirring bacon in a frying pan, and I got up and poured me a cup of coffee and poured a little bit of the whiskey we had left in it.

"Shorty, you want a little eye-opener?" I asked.

"Nope."

"You sure did have a good time last night, old son," I said and tried to laugh, but it made my head hurt.

Shorty didn't say a word. He just took the bacon out of the frying pan and sat down at the table and started eating.

"Shorty, who in the hell is Hamlet?"

"Dunno," he said.

"Well, last night you said you knew him well."

Shorty just kept on eating.

"And last night you called me a creamy-faced loon and run me out of the shack with a fire poker."

Shorty finished eating and started washing the dishes.

Well, I seen it won't be no use in talking about last night. Shorty just acted like it never happened.

We made the rest of the winter, and when the spring came, we packed up and headed down with me still doing all the talking.

When we got back to headquarters, Shorty packed up his outfit, drew his pay and lit out. I never did see him again, but every Christmas Eve I can't help remembering that night in the line shack when Shorty Pollard broke his silence.

Lacy Mallard

NOW, I COULDN'T swear that it was the gospel, but as far as I know, nobody never did see Lacy Mallard with his hat off. He wore all kinds of hats from time to time, but mostly he wore an old engineer's cap, pulled down on his head till it clean bent his ears.

He worked at Buchanon Brick and Tile. I'm talking about several years ago, before they had them fancy natural gas-fired kilns with all that uptown automated equipment. I mean, this was back in the days when they had them old round coal-fired kilns, and it used to get up to 150 degrees on them boys pulling bricks out.

Oh, they'd cool it down as much as they could, but you couldn't wait all day to take them new bricks out. So they'd pull off their hats, roll up their sleeves, put on a pair of flat rubber pieces that just covered the palms of their hands, and commence to pulling bricks.

That is, everybody but Lacy. Oh, he'd roll up his sleeves and put them rubber pieces on his hands, but Lacy Mallard won't about to take his hat off. No sir, no way, no time, no how.

And woe be unto the feller that tried to pull it off his head. Lacy stood six feet even, weighed about 190, and the muscles in his arms were as hard as steel. He'd been known to take on as many as three at a time, and he never once lost his hat. He broke Frank Hutchin's arm one time for messing with his hat. I mean, he didn't break it clean in two, but he sure give it a damn good fracture.

A bunch of us boys went swimming down at the river one day, and Lacy went with us. When we got there and everybody started putting on their bathing suits, Lacy said, "What are you doing?" We answered that we was putting on our bathing suits. Lacy laughed and said, "I ain't never owned a bathing suit in my life."

"Well," we said, "there ain't nobody here but us boys, so you can just swim naked."

He started taking his clothes off and we was all goggle-eyed, thinking that he was going to take that cap off. He took off his shoes and socks, his shirt, his pants, his underwear, and then he jumped in the water. I'll be a son of a bitch if that old engineer's cap didn't stay on his head like it was glued, never even moved, and he swam for two hours.

Somebody at work one day decided just to ask him to take his hat off, and Lacy told him, "My head ain't no damn show," and the other feller just kind of shriveled up.

I remember one time somebody talked Lacy into coming to church. He sat on the very back row, and he was dressed real nice, but he had a Budweiser beer cap on his head and he didn't take it off.

Everybody was looking at Lacy, more than they were

looking at Reverend Roe. The children were giggling, the men were snickering, and most of the women were giving him real dirty looks.

It was downright disrupting, but old Lacy sat there just as calm as a dead fish.

It was before the preaching started, when the choir was singing, and they were making announcements and things like that. Well, Reverend Roe stood up and said, "Mr. Mallard, we're glad to have you at church today." Lacy nodded. "And Mr. Mallard, it is customary and desired that upon entering the church, you remove your hat."

Lacy spoke right up and said, "Why?"

Reverend Roe was still smiling, but he kinda sputtered, "Why, why, you're just supposed to, that's all. Everybody does."

"Now, I ain't meaning no disrespect, Reverend, but I bet you can't show me in that Bible where it's a sin for a man to wear a hat in church. In fact, I hear that Jewish churches require it."

Mrs. Allie Barber was the waggingest-tongued woman you ever seen. I mean, she was a bun-headed, fire-and-brimstone mama that was about the size of a Kelvinator refrigerator, and her bosoms were as big as basketballs. She was a tattletale old biddy who claimed to be a saint, and she was the self-appointed guardian of the morals of Lee County. Anyway, she stood up and said, "How dare you to come into the company of Christian people and argue with the preacher, you hypocrite."

Well, that stung old Lacy Mallard, and he turned like he was heading for the door. The church was deathly quiet.

Uncle Woodrow Biddle was eighty-eight years old, and everybody in town loved and respected him. The old man hobbled to his feet and said, in his old cracked voice, "I hope that the Lord will forgive us for low-rating a man that wanted to come and worship with us. We ought to be ashamed of ourselves. I, for one, am, and I'm gonna walk back there and shake his hand." And the old man walked all bent over, with his walking stick, to the back of the church and shook Lacy's hand.

There wasn't a dry eye in the place and everybody went back and shook Lacy's hand, and they made him come sit right up on the front row and asked him to help take up collection and all. They just couldn't do enough for Lacy Mallard.

That was the best meeting I believe I've ever been to.

After service, Reverend Roe called Lacy off to the side and said, "Brother Mallard, we'll see you next Sunday. Uh, by the way, could you wear something that doesn't advertise beer?"

"Well, Reverend Roe, I'm mighty sorry. I plumb forgot about what this old cap had wrote on it. I'll wear a different one next Sunday. Good sermon."

And old Lacy was just as good as his word, cause Friday evening, after he got paid, he went down to J.C. Penney's in Sanford and got him one of them black felt baseball caps without nothing wrote on it. That was his Sunday hat and he wore it to church for a while, but then one Sunday he showed up in the prettiest pearl gray Stetson I've ever seen. Lacy Mallard had got religion.

I guess it goes without saying that there was all kinds of speculation about why Lacy Mallard wouldn't take his hat off. The most popular one was that he was baldheaded. Some people said that he had a big ugly scar on top of his head. Somebody said he was born real flat-headed and that he looked like Frankenstein if he took his hat off. You could hear all kinds of things.

When Lacy was called up to do jury duty, he ended up paying a fine for contempt of court because he wouldn't take that damn hat off.

Now, Lacy Mallard was not a drinking man. Oh, he might drink a little bit of homemade wine at Christmas time or a couple of beers once in a while, but that was it.

Well, some of us boys got to drinking and cutting up one night, and somebody come up with the idea that if we could manage to get Lacy drunk enough to pass out, that we could take his hat off and look at the top of his head. We decided that if we got the chance, we'd try it.

Buchanon Brick and Tile was having a big Fourth of July whoop-de-do for all the employees, and we decided that that would be as good a place as any to get old Lacy drunk.

When Lacy got there, somebody took him to the bushes right away. The bushes is where all the beer and whiskey was hid. See, in a dry county, the law don't care how much you drink as long as you keep it out of sight, and we were keeping it out of sight.

I guess it was just plain dirty what we done. I've been kinda ashamed of it every since. But anyway, what we done is, Glen Wheeler brought a bottle of vodka, and the first beer we give Lacy had a shot of it in it, and the second one had two. You can't taste vodka in beer worth a flip, and the drunker you get, the less you can taste.

After the third beer, Lacy said, "Boys, I'm not a heavy drinker, so I'd better quit."

"Hey, come on, Lacy," we all said. "It's the Fourth of July. Let's drink to the good old Stars and Stripes." Now, nobody couldn't refuse that, not in Lee County, North Carolina, on the Fourth of July.

So Lacy drank a beer with two and a half shots of vodka in it. Then we drank to George Washington and his brave soldiers crossing the Delaware, four shots, and by the time we got around to Nathan Hale, Glen had run out of vodka.

We was all pissy-eyed drunk and Lacy Mallard acted like he hadn't drunk a drop.

I mean, we was a mess. We was falling all over the place, and then we got real serious. Somebody started to sing "America the Beautiful," and Farrell Clemmons started crying. I don't mean he just had tears in his eyes. He was boo-hooing like a baby.

And then Ralph Aikens passed out, and Skeeter Goings threw up. Then we got the bright idea of jumping in the river to sober up, and we'd all drowned if it hadn't a-been for Lacy.

I guess the water sobered us up enough to get back to the picnic, and we was the sloppiest looking bunch you ever hope to see, wet clothes and all. Herbert Hart had lost one of his shoes and Cecil Oldham had mud all over him. We was a sight—that is, all but Lacy.

You talk about a mad bunch of womenfolks. Whew! All you could hear was, "Elmer, you do this every year," and "Clyde Bradford, you're a fine sight for your children to see."

But Lacy Mallard wasn't married and he didn't have to put up with it.

Most of us boys, Lacy included, belonged to the Wood-men of the World. We was getting excited because the annual convention was coming up in Atlanta, and we was all going. We was down at Gaddy's Tonsorial Parlor and

Barber Shop about a week before the convention, talking about it.

"Hot damn, didn't we have a good time in Myrtle Beach last year?"

"If Blanche had a-seen me in that place with them go-go girls, she'd a-had a hissie."

"Somebody told me that Clarence Fry from over at Southern Pines found one of them sporting girls and took her up to his room. Boy, they said that she was real pretty, and that she done everything but swallow the television set."

"Hot damn, I reckon! I wish that had a-been me."

Lacy hadn't said a word, and I figured it was because he hadn't never been to a Woodmen of the World convention before. Hell, I hadn't never been to one neither.

Somebody said, "Lacy, what do you think about them sporting girls?"

Lacy's face turned as red as the inside of a September watermelon, and he didn't say a word.

We left Friday evening right after work. We stopped at Cameron and picked up a case of beer, and we was on our way to Atlanta in Morris Butler's Ford with the two four-barrel carburetors, and McCalley Dowless's hot, candy-apple red Chevrolet.

We was eating up everything on the highway, and then we hit one of them radar traps, and McCalley got a ticket for doing ninety-five miles an hour, except that the old boy that give him the ticket was a right nice feller. He just wrote him up a ticket for seventy miles an hour, and we had to stop in Spartanburg and pay it.

We soft-footed it till we got out of South Carolina.

As soon as we crossed the Georgia line, we stopped and

157

got another case of beer and a pint of Colonel Lee and started picking up speed again.

Well, pretty soon, we was involved in a pretty good little run with a Dodge Dooley pickup truck that could run like a striped-ass ape. Me and Lacy both was riding with Morris Butler and pretty soon he buried the speedometer needle.

Lacy leaned up to the front seat and said, "Slow this son of a bitch down, Morris!"

Morris said, "But I'm beating him, Lacy!"

"Morris, I said to slow this son of a bitch down."

Well, Morris just took his foot off the gas and let her back down to seventy right quick, and he didn't bitch about it neither.

I mean, Lacy was just that way. He was a real good feller and didn't have a whole lot to say. But when he did say something, he meant it. Right up to and including fighting about it.

And another good thing about Lacy—he didn't hold no grudges. He went over to Frank Hutchin's place, after he broke Frank's arm, and split firewood for two evenings after he got off work.

Anyway, we got to Atlanta about six o'clock in the morning, feeling like sacks of horse manure. We hadn't been to sleep and was hung over. Lacy got us registered into the hotel, and this feller took our suitcases up to the room and showed us how the air conditioner worked and got us some ice and turned on the television for us.

We give him a tip and he said, "Thank you, gentlemen. If you need anything at all, please feel free to call the front desk. Enjoy your stay." And he was gone.

We piled into bed and slept for a few hours and woke up

raring to go. Lacy even acted like he wanted to get a look at Atlanta, so we all met down in the lobby.

"What do y'all want to do?"

"I'm hungry."

"Screw being hungry. You can be hungry at home."

"Let's get a drink."

"Yeah, I want a drink."

"Hot damn, I don't know if Atlanta is ready for us."

"Reckon there's any of them go-go girl places in Atlanta, Marvin?"

Some of them places we went in, a drink of whiskey cost three dollars and a half. And then we went in a go-go girl place, and they charged us five dollars just to get through the door, and the drinks were five dollars a piece.

Hot damn, it was worth it, though. This big tall girl come out in a brassiere and a little biddy thing around her bottom. She got right up in front of Herbert Hart and wiggled and shook right in his face.

As soon as the go-go girls got through dancing, we got up and left before we had to buy another five dollar drink.

We stopped at a liquor store and picked up two fifths of sourmash. Lacy said he figured he'd go on to bed, but everybody else come up to me and Marvin's room, and we got down to some pretty serious drinking.

We was in a high old mood. "Did you see her shaking it right in Herbert's face? I thought old Herbert was gonna reach right up there and grab ahold of that thing."

"How about us getting us one a them sporting girls?"

"Where do you get them at?"

"I don't know."

"Hey, that little feller that toted our suitcases up to the room said that if we needed anything at all to call the front desk.''

"Well, call 'em.''

"Hell, I ain't gonna call 'em.''

"Well, I sure ain't gonna call 'em.''

"Hell, give me another drink and I'll call 'em.

"Hello, can I talk to the front desk? . . . Thank you, ma'am . . . Hello, front desk? We're looking for a sporting girl . . . you know, a sporting girl . . . you know, one of them girls that comes up to the room and does stuff . . . you know, one of them girls that does stuff in bed . . . No, ma'am, I didn't mean . . . no, ma'am, don't call no police, we was just joking anyway. Goodbye. Well, they damn sure ain't got no sporting girls at the front desk. That woman talked to me like a dog.''

We had to go to some kind of meeting the next morning, and it was the silliest thing I ever been to. We all slipped out about halfway through—that is, all of us did but Lacy. He stayed till the last dog died.

Anyway, we headed on down the street and went in this bar and started getting wobbly-ass drunk.

I don't really like to drink with Herbert Hart. When he gets drunk, he gets belligerent. The first thing Herbert done was to call this feller a fat-ass fool. And the second thing Herbert done was to push this feller away from the jukebox.

And the next thing Herbert done was hit the floor. I mean, this feller popped Herbert upside of the head, and he went down like a two-hundred-pound sack of fertilizer.

Well, that knocked the fight out of Herbert Hart. He got up and took off running, and everybody else did, too. That is, everybody else but me, cause the biggest son of a bitch I ever laid eyes on had me around the neck. I couldn't holler. Hell, I couldn't hardly breathe, and I watched the rest of my friends run out the front door, probably thinking I was with them.

Well, this big dude had me by the neck and was almost lifting me off the floor. So I reached out and kicked him real hard right in the gonads. Well, he turned aloose of me right quick. He doubled over, and I knew he was gonna be out of commission for a while.

You know, I almost got out of that place, and then it all hit the fan. Somebody grabbed me by the arm, and there were three more closing in on me. I thought I was a goner.

And then I seen the prettiest sight I'd seen in a long time. It was Lacy Mallard, all dressed up and wearing his pearl gray Stetson, coming through the door under a full head of steam with blood in his eye.

He grabbed ahold of one feller and threw him down on the floor, and then he hit another feller so hard that I thought he had broke his neck.

I won't exactly loafing myself. I stomped this one feller's toe and then I kneed him in the belly. That left two, and Lacy had one of them by the head and the other one was chasing me around with a beer bottle.

Somehow or 'nother, I got ahold of a pool cue, and then I flat-out got the jump on him. I was just getting ready to cold-cock him with that pool cue when out of the corner of my left eye I seen that the feller that Lacy had ahold of had reached up and grabbed Lacy's pearl gray Stetson, and it was coming off his head.

Everything went into slow motion, and I watched in intense fascination as that pearl gray Stetson came floating off Lacy's head.

I could almost see the top of Lacy Mallard's head. It

was, it was . . . Blam! I got hit right between the eyes with a Schlitz beer bottle, and I was down for the count.

I woke up out on the sidewalk with Lacy carrying me. The first thing I done was to look up to see if Lacy had his hat on. He did. And my head hurt even worse.

Lacy Mallard got married last year, and him and his wife are expecting their first baby. There's people around here laying even money that it'll be born wearing a hat.

Honky-Tonk Avenue

EVERY BIG CITY has one. It may be called the block, the combat zone or some other colorful name that the locals have tacked on to it through the years, but no matter — it's the same few blocks of backstreet somewhere in the city, where the lonely go to buy company and the swingers and the hustlers parade up and down the concrete under gaudy signs advertising adult books, go-go girls, sex shows and bars. It's Bust-Out Junction. It's Down Street, USA. It's Honky-Tonk Avenue.

It's dressed up and it's nude. It's a loud jukebox or a soft whisper in the ear. It's brassy and bawdy and bad, and busting at the seams with that other life, those other people. Sometimes I wonder if they're really so different. Yes, I guess they are, in their own way.

But you take that lady standing in that shadowy doorway. She comes from one of the oldest families in Boston.

And that old man on the sidewalk snuggled up with a bottle of wine. Hell, he was a flyer in World War II. An ace, too. Ask him to show you his medals sometime. They're all he's got left.

And that wrinkled-up character behind the cash register in the uptown pool room. He's been sitting in that same spot for thirty years. People say he's a millionaire but just too greedy to enjoy it, so he sits there year after year in that same old felt hat with that stub of a cigar in his mouth. Maybe he's found a way to take it with him.

And that guy in the oversized overcoat and the dirty army cap. Don't pay too much attention to him. He's crazy. He wanders around all day looking for someone named Elaine.

And that dude on the corner in the floppy leather hat. Watch out for him. He's an undercover narc. You can always pick them out. They always wear floppy leather hats.

Down here you can buy a drink, a fix, or cold kisses from a painted lady of the evening. You can find a crap game or a fist fight. It's all here if you've got the price, and the price is never too high. High rollers just don't come down this far. This is the bottom.

We'd just had a big vice bust, and things were kinda quiet on the street the night that William Jonathan Cord came into our lives.

Billy Cord was from Wyoming, and he'd come to town to make it as a guitar player. But when he got here, he found out that guitar players are fifty cents a dozen in the big city. The gigs were few and far between, and when his funds were all gone, he drifted down to our neck of the woods looking for a job and a cheap hotel room.

As it turned out, he got both. Not much of a job, playing for strippers at the Scheherazade Club, but it was eating-money.

He was a nice enough kid and really looked out of place, thrown in with the motley cast of characters on the street. He always seemed amazed by what went on around him. He was young and wide-eyed and took life real personal. He was naive and innocent, and I guess that's why Big Sally took him under her wing. Sally runs the Scheherazade Club, and when you talk about a tough old bitch, Big Sally fits the bill.

She was hard-core personified and could bounce drunks with the best of them, but I guess the kid somehow brought out the mothering instincts in her. She gave him a job and a room and told the B-girls and other assorted hustlers to leave him alone.

The kid had talent, too. He could make that guitar talk, and in between the bump and grind of the strip shows, he'd play some of the songs he'd written himself. And fine songs they were, too, reminiscent of wide open spaces and clean air. And he could sing the old songs with his own flair and style.

He soon became a favorite with us. The darling of downtown. Bard of the boulevard, for what it was worth, and Honky-Tonk Avenue took him to its seedy bosom with something akin to love.

He was a sucker for a hard luck story, and he got the chance to hear plenty of them. He was always good for a cup of coffee or a bottle of Sneaky Pete, and his sympathetic ear got bent constantly.

The trouble started on a Saturday night when a bunch of punks from the other side of town came slumming. They didn't come to have fun; they came to belittle and laugh and harrass.

Old Major came shuffling up the street. He had the

Charlie Daniels

shakes and needed a drink real bad. He asked them for a few pennies to help him buy a bottle, and they gave him three dollars. The old man was beside himself and hurried into Manny's Liquor Store and came out with a bottle of Wild Irish Rose. When he came out, they followed him, and as soon as he broke the seal one of them jerked the bottle out of his hand and smashed it on the sidewalk. Old Major started crying and fell down on the ground.

One of them said, "Now, ain't that a shame. Here, old man, have a drink anyway," and shoved his face down into the broken glass. He got cut up pretty bad. A wino's blood is so thin from the constant alcohol that it flows like water, and they hurried away leaving the old man on the sidewalk bleeding like a sieve.

A couple of blocks down the street, Rose was standing in the doorway of the walk-up hotel plying her trade. "Hey, boys, want to have some fun?"

"How much for all of us at once?"

"Well, that's a pretty tall order, but I'm sure we could work something out. Come on upstairs and let's talk about it."

I won't go into what happened, but it was ugly. Rose was in the hospital for six weeks and was never to stand in her doorway again.

When they hit the street, they ran into Billy, guitar case in hand on his way to do the late show.

"Hey, hot shot, you a guitar player?"

"Yeah," Billy said, flashing them his best smile.

"Well, take that guitar out and play us a song."

"I don't have time," Billy said, still smiling, "but come on down to the Scheherazade and I'll play you a bunch of songs."

"No, here! You'll play right here for us."

They were high on cocaine and spoiling for a fight, so Billy said OK, unpacked his guitar and played a song.

When he finished, one of them said, "Now, I don't think that was worth a damn! If you can't play any better than that, you don't deserve that guitar. Give it to me!"

Billy said, "Now boys, I don't want any trouble. I'm late for work. Why don't you come on down to the Scheherazade and I'll buy you all a drink?"

"Give me that guitar," said the leader.

Billy fought hard, but there were just too many of them. They took his guitar and smashed it against a light pole. Then they started smashing on him. They left him lying in an alley, out cold.

Now, you may think that there is no honor among people like us. You may think that you can't degrade a person who's just about as far down as he can go. But you'd be wrong.

Within a few minutes, the word had spread up and down the street like wildfire: We were under attack. It wasn't the first time it had happened and probably wouldn't be the last, but even bums have pride.

Big Sally put the word out, and we came as fast as we could. Sam the Bouncer with his brass knuckles, Willie the Pool Hustler with a straight razor in his pocket, the girls from the bawdy house on the corner carrying anything from razor blades to hatpins. We were all there, an army of misfits in cast-off clothes, smelling of rot-gut whiskey and cheap perfume.

Sally stood up and cleared her throat. "Old Major's dead, Rose is on her way to the hospital, and they stomped Billy's hands and broke his fingers and busted his guitar."

Charlie Daniels

I could have sworn I saw a tear glisten in that faded granite eye.

"You all know the story. Ain't no sense in calling the law. They ain't gonna do nothing anyway."

"Bunch of punks looking for trouble."

"Well, let's go give 'em some."

We went out the back and down the alley. A sideshow of freaks and riffraff reaching out for a tiny speck of dignity.

A shadow flitted out of an alleyway, and a hoarse whisper touched the midnight air. "They're in Little John's bustin' up the place. The back door's open."

"Come on." Sally headed down the alley toward the back of Little John's Booze and Blues Tavern. She inched the back door open and we all slipped through as quiet as we could.

There were six of them, mostly big guys. You know the type. They run in packs, like wolves, only picking on the helpless. Spoiled brats, high on daddy's money, big men on campus.

As we went through the back door, the wolves had the place under siege. Poor old John was lying on his back on the bar. Two of them held him while another one poured whiskey in his face. He was about to drown, coughing and sputtering. The others had Maggie, the waitress, down on the floor behind the pool table. The few customers had left when they came in, so there was nobody else in the place.

As we went through the back door, Benny the Dip came through the front door, closed and locked it and stood there with a length of pipe in his hand.

The punks were so high and so intent on tormenting the bartender and waitress that they didn't even see us coming. Somebody, I don't remember who it was, started it off by hitting one of the guys holding John full in the face with half a pool cue. He was down for the count with his nose spurting blood like a fountain.

Suddenly Willie's razor was against the throat of another one. "How'd you like to breathe through your neck, boy?" The boy didn't move a muscle and his eyes held the fear of a rat cornered by a rattlesnake.

Benny the Dip waded in with his pipe on the ones behind the pool table, and before anybody knew what happened, they were all on the floor, except the one who seemed to be the ringleader, and he was standing behind the bar all alone.

"If you touch me, my Daddy will have you put in jail for a hundred years," he blustered, trying to look mean and tough.

Big Sally stepped up and faced him, and the look on her face was scary to see. "Daddy ain't gonna even know what happened to you, boy. You ain't leaving here. You're gonna die right where you stand," and a snub-nosed .38 pistol appeared in her hand.

He fell apart quick. He started crying and trembling. "We didn't mean no harm. We were just having fun. We'll pay for all the damage."

"You damn right you'll pay, boy. Put your hands on the bar."

Like a whipped puppy, the boy laid his hands on the bar. Sally held the gun in her left hand and reached for Benny's lead pipe with the right.

"What I really want to do is kill you, boy. If you so much as move a muscle, I'm gonna put some hot lead right between your eyes."

So saying, she brought the lead pipe down hard on one

Charlie Daniels

of his hands. He screamed like a banshee and almost jerked the ruined hand off the bar, but the look in Big Sally's eyes made him leave it there.

Sally's face was cold. "Now the other one, big man. You can dish it out, but let's see how you can take it." She brought the pipe down on his other hand and he passed out, falling to the floor behind the bar.

The other five had been watching in horrified fascination, and now she turned her cold, cold eyes on them and they shivered.

One by one, they were led before the bar.

"You like to pour whiskey, don't you punk? Hand me a fifth of bourbon." Sally uncorked the bottle and we forced the boy to his knees.

"Boy, you're gonna have a drink, a big drink," she said, handing him the bottle.

"You drink it all, boy, every drop, and if you take that bottle down from your mouth before it's empty, I'm gonna make you a new belly-button about the size of a .38 bullet."

I've seen some awesome drinking in my time, but I've never seen anybody drink a whole bottle of whiskey before. He drank that whole fifth without taking the neck of the bottle out of his mouth. He was violently sick and rolled around on the floor like a chicken with its neck wrung.

The next one was dragged up facing her on his knees. "You're kinky, ain't you, boy? You like to molest little girls behind pool tables. Come here, Myrtle, and give me that long hatpin."

She held the gun against his temple. "Keep your hands behind you, boy, if you want to live."

170

She jabbed the hatpin through his right jaw. He howled and cried for mercy, but there was no mercy in Big Sally's face as she pushed the hatpin through his mouth and out through the other cheek.

The next one had the finest head of hair I ever did see. It was razor cut, and you could tell he spent a lot of time combing it.

"You've got pretty hair, but it's styled all wrong. Willie, bring your razor over here and give pretty boy a haircut."

Willie shaved his head just as clean as a whistle, with no soap, no water, no nothing, and all the time Sally had that gun barrel touching his nose.

The other two were brought up together. "You big-time lovers ought to display your wares. Take your clothes off, gentlemen."

Off came the clothes, all of them, socks, underwear, everything. "Now hit the street." And they were shoved out the front door trying to cover themselves with their hands.

Sally turned back to the others, and a sniveling, sorry-looking bunch they were. "You punks hurt some good people tonight, and in the process you killed a harmless old man. You might have done him a favor, but it's not your place to decide who lives and dies. Now, take your filth back across the tracks and you'd better not even look back, or we'll see if the police are interested in this matter. If you ever set foot on this street again, you'll go back in a hearse."

Just like that, it was over, and they were unceremoniously pushed out the door. They must have had a hell of a time explaining when they got home.

Old Major was buried in an unmarked grave, alongside so many others who had gone on before, unknown and unmourned. The police asked a few questions, but they really didn't try too hard. It was just one less bum to have to deal with for them.

It was six weeks before Rose came back from the hospital with a long, disfiguring scar down the side of her face. Big Sally gave her a job bartending at the Scheherazade Club.

And poor Billy. The light was gone out of those blue eyes. He just lay in bed all day staring at his bandaged hands.

As time went by, his hands started healing, but his spirit didn't. Billy took to drinking, and every day he sank a little deeper in the mire of Honky-Tonk Avenue.

He got into fights and was jailed, and one night he passed out on the street and spent the night on the sidewalk. Sally had us pick him up the next morning. We cleaned him up and put him to bed, and when he woke up, she was sitting there.

"I want to talk to you, son," she said. "I've been sitting here thinking for hours, and I've got something to say to you. If you stay here much longer, you'll spend the rest of your life here. You're gonna end up on the corner begging for nickels. You can't beat this street, Billy. It'll drain you and drag you down. It'll beak your heart, and in the end it'll kill you. You don't belong here, son.

"You see, for most of us down here there's no place to go. We've hit the bottom and there's no ladder to climb out. We're stuck, but you're not. Not yet. But you will be if you stay. Oh, you can crawl into a bottle and watch the world fall down around you, and when that happens, you'll want to die. But you'll go on living, if you can call it living.

"I know all about that," Sally said. "I'm a hard old woman, but I haven't always been. There was a time when I had hopes and dreams, and there was a time when there was love in my life, but I let it all slip away. I let the world shove me into this little corner of hell.

"There's a whole world out there, son, a world with clean air and sunshine and children, and you're a part of that world. Go on back to Wyoming, Billy. You don't belong here. I've known it since the first day you came here. I should have sent you away then, but you're the first person I've been able to love in thirty years. It'd break my heart to see you end up in this hellhole, rotting your insides on cheap wine and lying around in the gutter. Go home, son."

Billy put his arms around the old woman, and they held on to each other for a long time.

Everybody chipped in to buy Billy a going-away present. Some of us could only contribute a few cents, but we came up with the money somehow.

The day he left, we were all at Big Sally's to say goodbye, and when she gave him the guitar, his eyes moistened. He tuned it and his fingers were stiff, but they loosened up as he went along.

"It's almost time for your bus, Billy. Sing me that song you wrote about Wyoming before you go," Sally said.

And he sang it like never before. And when he finished, there wasn't a dry eye in the house.

He packed his new guitar and went around the room hugging everybody. When he finished, he said, "I know that the rest of the world looks down on you people, but to me you're the salt of the earth. Wherever I go, whatever I do, you'll always be in my heart. You'll always be a part of my family." His voice cracked and he said, "I love you, everyone. May God bless you."

He embraced Sally, kissed her on both cheeks and was gone.

That's been a few years back. The pool room burned down last May. Benny the Dip is back in prison again, and Sally passed away in her sleep last week.

We buried her with the picture, the one that Billy sent her of him, his wife and his little girl, the one inscribed, "With Love to Grandma Sally, from little Sally."

People come and people go. The seasons change, the earth spins and death goes relentlessly on and on, but this street never really changes.

Not that it's so unique. Every big city has one. It's Bust-Out Junction. It's Down Street, USA. It's Honky-Tonk Avenue.

The Legend Of Wooley Swamp

MY PATERNAL GRANDMOTHER lived to be eighty-seven years old. A righteous woman, quick of step and bright of eye, her mind stayed as sharp as a steel trap right up through her last years. She lived just down the road from us, and I used to spend a lot of time with her.

I loved to hear her talk about the old days, when my grandfather used to come courting on a fine bay gelding, riding five miles over and five miles back. My grandfather had passed away a few years before, but my grandmother talked about him as if he were still alive.

"Oh, you should have seen him, Davey boy," she'd say. "He could ride like the wind, was as strong as an ox and as handsome as any man."

And it was all true. My grandfather was a minor legend around Bladen County. I've heard a lot of the old-timers talk about his great strength, about his gargantuan capacity for moonshine whiskey, and about the brawls he was involved in up and down the length and breadth of the county.

175

But that was all before he was converted and lived the last years of his life as a devout Baptist, deacon in the church, and a hard-working tobacco farmer.

My grandmother, in her youth, had been a strikingly beautiful girl, as was attested to by the pictures in the family album, and according to all the old folks, her favor had been much sought after.

My grandfather, who was considered a right rakish and unstable character by the good people of Bladen County at that time, first saw her when she was out on a Sunday afternoon drive in Lucius Clay's spoke-wheeled buggy. She was seventeen years old, and when he saw her for the first time, he almost fell off his horse. He finally did when he started showing off, jumping his horse over fences and other such foolishness. If the truth be known, he'd probably had more than his share of the jug that him and his buddies were nipping on.

Lucius Clay, who was the leading suitor in my grandmother's life at that time, was a teller in the bank at Elizabethtown. He was said to live up to his Scottish heritage. People used to say that he could squeeze a nickel until the buffalo hollered. But thrift was considered a virtue in that day and time, and Lucius Clay was considered an up-and-coming young man.

Needless to say, my grandmother's first impression of my grandfather was somewhat less than favorable. She tossed her head at his antics and laughed out loud when he fell off his horse. But my grandfather's Irish spirit was undaunted, and he declared to his running mates that this was the girl he would marry.

One night the following week, he came riding up to my grandmother's gate, dressed up like a dandy in a pinchback suit and smelling of lilac water. He tied his horse to the fence and walked up to the door just as bold as you please, where my grandmother and Lucius Clay were sitting on the front porch swing.

"Good evening, Miss Mollie. Evening, Lucius."

"What are you doing here, Conner MacDaniels?" Lucius Clay asked, more than a little irritated.

My grandfather, never one to be bashful, spoke right up and said, "Why, the same as you, Lucius. I came to see this charming lady."

"Well, she don't want to see the likes of you," Lucius declared.

"Let the lady speak for herself," my grandfather said firmly.

"Now, gentlemen, let's be sociable. Mr. MacDaniels is welcome to sit for a spell if he'd like," my grandmother said, trying to smooth things over.

And sit a spell he did, and fairly took over the conversation, making my grandmother smile and giggle, much to Lucius Clay's consternation.

From that night on, it was all downhill for Lucius Clay. My grandmother was so taken with my grandfather's easy manner and quick wit that Lucius Clay just kind of faded out of the picture.

They were married the next spring, and went on to live a long and fruitful life together.

Now, my grandmother was a master storyteller, and all master storytellers tend to let the years color any story to some extent, but this is the way she told it to me.

After being spurned by my grandmother, Lucius Clay seemed to lose all interest in romance. In fact, he lost all interest in everything except making and keeping money.

177

Charlie Daniels

He scrimped and saved, becoming more and more of a recluse. A few years later, he quit his job at the bank and used the money he had accumulated to buy mortgages on farms that he eventually foreclosed on — all legal but heartless, to say the least, putting a lot of people out in the cold without a roof over their heads. He then sold these properties for enormous gains and reinvested and doubled his profits many times over.

And Lucius Clay didn't keep one cent in the bank. Nobody knew where he kept his money, but it was rumored that he had it all in cash, and that he used to sit around and fondle it and let it sift through his fingers.

As the years went by, Bladen County saw less and less of Lucius Clay, and when they did he looked more and more like a bum. He dressed in worn-out old clothes and lived in one room in a big two-story house that was so run-down it looked abandoned. People used to say that he was just too stingy to do any different.

When the Great Depression hit, our little county was no different from the rest of the country. Our bank failed, leaving the people with money in it completely broke. Everybody was having a hard time, and nobody had any cash money to speak of. That is, nobody but Lucius Clay. And what he had, he kept hidden.

Bladen County, being only about fifty miles from the Atlantic Ocean, really catches it during a hurricane, and during one particular bad storm the roof was completely torn off the First Baptist Church. The membership was in a quandary. Nobody had money to help have it fixed. The deacons were called together at Reverend Meek's house to try to come up with a plan, and somebody got the bright idea to ask Lucius Clay to open up his heart and help to replace the church roof.

"You know he's got the money."

"He's a member of the community."

"He can't be that tight," they rationalized. So it was decided that Reverend Meeks would head a committee to go out to see Mr. Clay and enlist his help.

Southern people are notorious for tagging things and places with colorful names. The section that Lucius Clay's house was situated in had been known as Booger Woods for as long as anyone could remember. It was at the edge of a most fearful place known as Wooley Swamp.

They drove out to see Lucius on a beautiful spring afternoon. They knocked on the front door of the dilapidated old house but got no answer. They went around to the back and knocked on the back door. Still no answer. They were just about to give up and go back to town when Lucius came walking out of the deep woods carrying a shovel and looking just about as glad to see them as he would've if they'd been werewolves.

"Brother Clay, how nice to see you," Reverend Meeks said, reaching out his hand.

Lucius neither offered to shake his hand nor return the greeting.

"This here is private property. Y'all ain't got no business out here bothering with me," Lucius Clay declared.

"Brother Clay, we've come to enlist your help in a holy cause," the good reverend said. "As I'm sure you know, our First Baptist Church is the oldest church in the county and one of the oldest churches in the state of North Carolina. Well, the hurricane we had the other night has torn the roof completely off, and we're asking you, as a member of the community, to make a donation to help replace

179

the roof. We felt that you'd want to, seeing as how so many of your friends attend church there. Now, we need $5,000, and as much of that figure as you could see your way clear in giving us would be most appreciated."

"Why can't you people leave me alone? I moved out of your damn town, I don't bother with none of you, and I want you to get off of my property and leave me alone. I won't give you a red cent, not a red cent. My money belongs to me. Now, git!"

Needless to say, the reverend and deacons beat a hasty retreat. What else could they do?

That's the last time that anybody ever saw Lucius Clay. When he had not come into town for supplies in six months or so, fearing that the old man had died, the sheriff took it upon himself to investigate. He drove out to the spooky old house on the edge of Wooley Swamp and found absolutely no sign of Lucius Clay. The old house was empty, and a search of the grounds and woods turned up nothing.

There was a period of wild speculation, but soon even that died away, leaving the disappearance of Lucius Clay a mystery to be unsolved for all time.

Many is the person who went out to the old house in search of Lucius Clay's money. They fairly ripped the old place apart, dug up the yard, and searched high and low, netting not a farthing, and in a few years, they gave up.

There were a few wild rumors that him or his ghost had been seen around the old house one night carrying a lantern, but hardly anyone believed it.

Now, Wooley Swamp was probably the orneriest piece of real estate in our part of the world, or any place else for that matter. It was all overgrown with briars and thick underbrush and loaded with rattlesnakes, alligators, quicksand and all manner of forbidding things.

The only time anybody ever went there was in the dead of winter after the mosquitoes were gone and the rattlesnakes and alligators had holed up for the season. And even in cold weather, very few made the trip.

Rayford Bivens was said to have the finest bunch of coon dogs in the country. He bred and hunted bluetick hounds. He hunted hard from the first frost until the season closed in February. Rayford loved two things — coon hunting and white whiskey — and he used to combine the two on a regular basis. He was always telling lies about the size of the coons his dogs treed and just about anything else he deemed to talk about, for that matter. So when he told his Lucius Clay story, nobody believed him. That is, almost nobody.

He claimed that one night, when there was a full moon, his hounds had treed way back in Wooley Swamp. He swore that he had come across the old man, who had either been digging up or burying mason jars full of cash money. People wrote it off to an alcohol dream.

Jasper Cagle had the reputation for making the best bootleg whiskey to ever come out of Bladen County. He should have, because that's all he had ever done.

He lived with his three no-account sons — Palmer, Roscoe and Archie — over on Carver's Creek. They were a sorry lot, always getting into fights and all kinds of trouble. Palmer had pulled some time on the chain gang for cutting up a fellow at the pool room in Elizabethtown.

The story goes that one night when Rayford Bivens had dropped by to replenish his supply of drinking whiskey and remained to consume a good bit of it on the premises, he got to spouting off about his coon dogs and such, and eventually he drifted into the story about seeing Lucius Clay in the swamp with all that money.

The Cagle boys didn't pay much attention to him until he happened to mention that he had been in the vicinity of the old footpath that ran back into the swamp to an abandoned logging camp.

After Rayford Bivens left, Palmer called his other two brothers together and said, "Do y'all remember when the law got hot on us last winter, and Daddy had to move the still? Well, I helped him move it and we hid it about a mile back in Wooley Swamp up that old footpath. Well, I remember seeing a whole bunch of footprints all up and down that path. That old man might be back in there after all. We could slip back in there and take old Lucius's money and feed him to the alligators and nobody would ever know."

"Hell, Palmer, I ain't going back in that spooky old swamp," said Archie, the youngest of the brothers.

"You'll damn well do as I say," Palmer told him, giving him a resounding open-handed slap across the face.

Well, that settled that, and the next night, under a full moon, the Cagle boys started down the path that led to the depths of the dismal old swamp.

They walked for hours and were just about ready to give up and go home when they saw the tiniest glimmer of light about three hundred yards up the path.

"Let's go and be quiet," Palmer told them.

"I ain't a-going, Palmer. They said they's haints back in there," Archie whimpered.

"Shut up, you milk sop. There ain't no such thing as haints," Palmer said roughly, shoving the other two down the path.

They inched along ever so quiet until they were almost to the dim light. As they strained their eyes to see, they could make out the form of a man digging in the ground by lantern light.

"It's him, it's him," Roscoe whispered as the old man starting pulling jars out of the hole.

"Let's go," Palmer said, breaking cover and running full tilt up the path toward the old man. He never had a chance. Palmer ran up and kicked him in the side, and Roscoe picked up the old man's shovel and brought it down full-force across his head. Archie picked up a stout stick and started flailing away. The old man went limp, and they picked him up and threw him into the black water of the swamp.

"We're rich, we're rich," they all chimed in, picking up the mason jars full of money and dancing around with absolutely no remorse.

"Let's count it."

"No, let's get the hell out of here and then we'll count it."

"We're rich, we're rich! I'm gonna buy me a brand-new automobile."

"I'm gonna get me a whole closet full of fancy clothes."

"We're rich!"

There were thirteen jars in all, stuffed with bills of every denomination and coins of every kind, even a few gold pieces.

There was an empty burlap bag lying on the ground, and they jerked it up, put the jars inside and headed back up the path.

"You know what I'm gonna do, Palmer? I'm gonna buy me a whole case of sardines and eat every one of them myself."

"I'm gonna buy me the fanciest pair of boots you ever did see."

"You two shut up and let's get home with this before daylight," Palmer said, hurrying along the path.

The full moon, which had been lighting the old foot path, suddenly went behind a cloud.

"I can't see a damn thing. We should have brought that lantern. Roscoe, go back and get it."

"You can beat me till your arms get tired, Palmer, and I ain't going back there by myself."

"Never mind, you lily-livered coward. We'll all go back." And they turned around and started back the other way, groping along in the dark.

They were almost back to where they'd left the lantern still burning on the ground. They could see it through the underbrush. Suddenly, the lantern moved. It rose up off the ground as if someone were carrying it.

The three boys watched in horror as it started down the path toward them, and then they ran back down the path as hard as they could go, bumping into trees and tearing their skin on briars and vines.

The burlap bag of money was dropped on the ground in their haste.

"The damn thing's gaining on us, Palmer."

"Palmer, get us out of here."

But Palmer had lost the path and was leading his two brothers through the swamp, and still the lantern came on.

"I'm stuck. I can't move my feet. Help me! Help me!" Archie was struggling, but the harder he struggled, the

184

deeper he sank. And then all three were struggling and screaming as the dreaded quicksand sucked them down.

Just before they went under, an eerie laugh as loud as thunder split the stillness of the deep swamp. It's the last thing they ever heard.

I used to shiver when my grandmother told me the last part. I could just see that lantern moving through the trees and feel the quicksand sucking at my feet. And I guess I even believed the story. But as I got older, I changed my mind.

Lucius Clay had been a real man. That much was true. He had been extremely greedy and had disappeared from the face of the earth. That much was also true. But everything else had been made up and enhanced — an old wives' tale from fifty years ago.

My grandmother used to end the story by saying, "And, Davey Boy, if you follow that old footpath back in the swamp on a night when the moon is full, you can still hear them Cagle boys screaming, and you can hear that old man laugh and see that lantern moving through the woods."

Rayford Bivens and Jasper Cagle had both died before I was born, and only the oldest residents of Bladen County even remembered the legend of Wooley Swamp.

My grandmother passed away when I was fourteen years old, and I all but forgot about the old story. As I grew into young manhood, other things like football and girls took my fancy and my energy. I did pretty well with the football, but the girls were another story. There was this one girl, Patty McClure, who to me was the most beautiful creature on earth. And the most unattainable. Every time I'd get around her, I'd almost lose my breath.

I was not the only one with eyes for Patty McClure. Half

Charlie Daniels

the boys in Mrs. Campbell's eighth grade class were head over heels in love with her.

I don't know if you remember what it was like being a fourteen-year-old boy growing up in a small town in the South, but I do. When you liked a girl, the thing to do was to "show off" around her. "Showing off" could entail anything from hitting a baseball over the outfielder's head, to throwing somebody down on the ground to show how strong you were, to bragging about anything outstanding you had done, from the truth to a downright lie.

Clayton Bell was my main competition for Patty McClure's attention, and it seemed like if I hit a triple, he'd hit a homerun. If I threw somebody down, then he'd do it faster and harder. And no matter how big a lie I told about something brave I'd done, he could tell a bigger one. Clayton was a downright pain.

One day in school, Mrs. Campbell had to go to the principal's office for some reason or other, leaving the class unattended for about fifteen minutes. I immediately went into my act. But I couldn't get to Patty's desk before that aggravating Clayton Bell had her cornered.

"Me and my brother went in the old Martin house one night," he bragged.

Patty responded. "Oh, Clayton, they say the old Martin house is haunted," she purred. "You must have been scared to death."

"Nah, it's just an old house, and besides, if it is haunted, I wouldn't be afraid anyway. There ain't no such thing as ghosts."

"Oh, Clayton, you must really be brave."

He was puffed up like a bullfrog and cast victorious eyes in my direction.

"Well, I ain't never found nothing that I'm afraid of. If you want to call that brave, I guess I am," he boasted.

That tore it for me. "Clayton Bell," I said, "you're afraid of your own shadow. Besides, everybody knows that the old Martin place ain't haunted. I've been in there lots of times at night, and there ain't a blamed thing scary about it." Which was a bald-faced lie. You couldn't have paid me to go near the old Martin place at night.

"Oh yeah?" he blustered. "Well, I've walked right through the Oak Hill graveyard right by myself at midnight," he countered.

"Well, that ain't so much. If you're so big and brave, why don't you walk through Wooley Swamp at midnight?"

"Well, I would if I wanted to, and since you're so almighty brave, why don't you?"

Patty McClure played us both like fish on a line. "Why don't you both?"

"I'll do it, but he won't," Clayton Bell said. "He's afraid to go out of the house at night."

"Oh yeah? Well, I'll go to Wooley Swamp just any old night you want to, Mr. Bell."

"There's gonna be a full moon tonight," Patty said, kind of coylike. I was wishing that she'd stay out of this.

"Well, it's all right with me."

"Me, too."

So there we stood with our backs to the wall. The object of our affection had pulled the plug. Put up or shut up.

"I'll meet you behind the courthouse at 11:30." Clayton Bell made it sound like a dare.

"I'll be there."

When Mrs. Campbell came back to class, of all things we read "The Legend of Sleepy Hollow." And it was the first time in my life that I wished school would last all day and all night.

After supper that night, I went up to my room and got in bed and turned out the light. A little while later, I heard Mama and Daddy go into their room across the hall. The Big Ben on the table beside my bed said ten o'clock. I never did see time go by so fast. It was 11:15 before I knew it.

I almost didn't go, but I got to thinking about Clayton's leering face in class the next day and got up and put my clothes on.

I grabbed Daddy's three-cell flashlight, raised my window, went out on the upstairs porch, and being as quiet as I could, shimmied down the big magnolia tree and headed for the courthouse, hoping against hope that Clayton Bell was at home in bed fast asleep.

Small towns retire early, and they rolled up the sidewalks in our town at ten o'clock on weeknights. With all the lights out and the streets deserted, our friendly little neighborhood looked eerie under the full moon.

I ran the three blocks to the courthouse and went around to the back. Clayton wasn't there. I rejoiced and took off for home, but I ran full-tilt into him on the courthouse lawn.

"Where you going, boy?" he said kinda tauntinglike.

"I didn't think you were coming and I was going home, that's where I was going. I've been waiting on you for a half hour," I lied.

"Well, let's go get this over with." And he started off down the street like he was John Wayne.

We made it to the edge of town in about fifteen minutes, and it must have been right at twelve o'clock when we came up on the edge of the swamp. The old footpath looked absolutely forbidding under the full moon.

Neither one of us said a word. We just walked down the path about thirty feet and stopped.

"Well, we did it," Clayton said. "Let's go." Now, I realized that we really hadn't gone back in Wooley Swamp, and he did too, but we both knew that when we got to school the next day we'd embellish the story to make it sound as if we'd walked all the way through it.

We turned around and started back when all of a sudden . . . that screech owl must have been right on top of us. We both took off running like our pants were on fire. We must have run for a mile. The trouble is that in our haste to get away, we ran the wrong way and here we were a mile back in Wooley Swamp, plumb out of breath, when we realized what we had done.

As we stood there getting our breath back so we could run some more, Clayton said, "Please don't run off and leave me." And then I realized that he was more scared than I was, if such a thing was possible. He was holding onto me in a death grip.

I guess seeing Clayton Bell fall apart gave me courage of a sort. "Oh, it's all right, Clayton," I said in my deepest voice. "That old screech owl just shook us up. We'll just walk on back out of here."

I'll swear I don't know to this day if we imagined it or if it really happened, but out of the corner of my eye I saw something flicker down in the swamp. When Clayton saw me looking in that direction, he looked and saw it, too.

It would appear and disappear, like somebody walking through the woods with a lighted lantern. It might have been swamp fire or it could have been lightning bugs, but I couldn't speak and my legs were made out of lead. I thought Clayton was gonna pass out. Every time we saw it, it seemed to get closer, but we were rooted to the spot, too terrified to move.

"Aiyehhiiaah!"

Something that sounded like somebody screaming split the night and hung on the midnight air. That unstuck our legs. We took off like a rocket, tripping over each other trying to get out of the swamp.

"Aiyehhiiaah!" again, and then, "Ha, ha, ha!" like somebody laughing in a deep bass voice. We ran and ran and ran. We were flying on the wings of fear. We didn't stop when we came out of the swamp. We didn't even stop when we hit town. I don't know how I did it, but I ran all the way home, with Clayton right on my heels, before I collapsed on our lawn.

Clayton was too scared to go home by hisself, so he climbed up the magnolia tree and spent the night with me. You should have seen me explaining that to my parents the next morning.

That's been a lot of years ago. Clayton Bell is an insurance salesman in Durham now. Patty McClure got married, got fat and had three children. And I'm still in Bladen County carrying on the family tradition of tobacco farming. And Wooley Swamp is still there, still as forbidding and sinister as ever.

I've never been back into the old swamp. It's not that I'm scared anymore, but as my grandmother used to say, "Davey boy, sometimes it's just better to let sleeping dogs lie."

A Carolina
Christmas Carol

I MIGHT AS well go ahead and tell you right up front: I believe in Santa Claus. Now, you can believe or not believe, but I'm here to tell you for a fact that there is a Santa Claus, and he does bring toys and stuff like that on Christmas Eve night.

I know, I know. It sounds like I've had too much eggnog, don't it? All I ask is that you wait till I get through telling my story before you make up your mind.

When I was a kid, Christmas time had a magic to it that no other season of the year had. There was just something in the air, something that you couldn't put your finger on, but it was there, and it affected everybody.

It seemed like everybody smiled and laughed more at that time of the year, even the people who didn't hardly smile and laugh the rest of the year.

"You reckon it's gonna snow? Boy, I sure do wish it'd snow this year. Do you reckon it's gonna?"

Heck no, it won't gonna snow. As far as I know, it ain't

never snowed in Wilmington, North Carolina, at Christmas time in the whole history of man. It seemed like everybody in the world had snow at Christmas except us.

In the funny papers, Nancy and Sluggo and Little Orphan Annie had snow to frolic around in at Christmas time. The Christmas cards had snow. Bing Crosby even had snow to sing about. But not one flake fell on Wilmington, North Carolina.

But that didn't dampen our spirits one little bit. Our family celebrated Christmas to the hilt. We were a big, close-knit family, and we'd gather up at Grandma's house every year. My grandparents lived on a farm in Bladen County, about fifty miles from Wilmington, and I just couldn't wait to get up there.

They lived in a great big old farmhouse, and every Christmas they'd fill it up with their children and grandchildren. We'd always stay from the night of the twenty-third through the morning of the twenty-sixth.

There'd be Uncle Clyde and Aunt Martha, Uncle Lacy and Aunt Selma, Uncle Leroy and Aunt Mollie, Uncle Stewart and Aunt Opal, and my mama and daddy, Ernest and Nadine. I won't even go into how many children were there, but take my word for it, there was a bunch.

There'd be people sleeping all over that big old house. We kids would sleep on pallets on the floor, and we'd giggle and play till some of the grown-ups would come and make us be quiet.

All the usual ground rules about eating were off for those days at Grandma's house. You could eat as much pie and cake and candy as you could hold, and your mama wouldn't say a word to you.

My Grandma would cook from sunup to sundown and

love every minute of it. She'd have cakes, pies, candy, fruit and nuts setting out all the time, and on top of that, she'd cook three big meals a day. I mean, we eat like pigs.

Christmas was also the only time that my Granddaddy would take a drink. It was a Southern custom of the time not to drink in front of small children, so Granddaddy kept his drinking whiskey hid in the barn. When he'd want to go out there and get him a snort, he'd say that he had to go see if the mare had had her foal yet.

It was a good, good time. A little old-fashioned by some people's standards, but it suited us just fine.

If I'm not mistaken, it was the year I was five years old that my cousin Buford told me that there wasn't any Santa Claus. Buford was about nine at the time. He always was a mean-natured cuss. Still is.

Well, I just refused to believe him. I said, "You're telling a great big fib, Buford Ray, cause Santa Claus comes to see me every Christmas, right here at Grandma and Granddaddy's house."

"That ain't Santa Claus. That's your mama and daddy."

One thing led to another and I got so upset about the prospect of no Santa Claus that I went running in the house crying.

"Grandma, Grandma! Buford says there ain't no Santa Claus! There is a Santa Claus, ain't they, Grandma?"

"Of course there is, Curtis. Buford was just joking with you."

Aunt Selma heard me talking to Grandma and walked to the door. "Buford Ray, get yourself in this house right this minute!"

When he came in, Aunt Selma grabbed him by the ear, led him into the front room and swatted him.

Charlie Daniels

Granddaddy was also a big defender of Santa Claus. He would talk about Santa Claus like he was a personal friend of his. And the more he went to check on the mare, the more he talked about Santa Claus, or "Sandy Claws," as he called him.

"Yes, children, old Sandy Claws will be hitching up them reindeers and heading on down this a-way before long. Wonder what he's gonna bring this year?"

He'd have us so excited by the time we went to bed that I reckon if visions of sugarplums ever danced in anybody's heads, it was ours.

Christmas Eve night, after we had eat about as much supper as we could hold, we'd go in the front room. There'd always be a big log fire crackling in the fireplace, and Granddaddy would always say the same thing.

"Children, do y'all know why we have Christmas every year?"

"Cause that's when the Baby Jesus was born."

"That's right. We're celebrating the Lord's birthday. Do y'all know where He was born at?"

"In Bethlehem," we would all chime in.

"That's right, He was born in a stable in Bethlehem almost two thousand years ago."

Then Granddaddy would put on his spectacles and read Saint Luke's version of the Christmas story. Then, after we'd had family prayer, Granddaddy would always get a twinkle in his eye. "I reckon I'd better step out to the barn and see if that old mare has had her baby yet."

There was always a chorus of, "Can I go with you, Granddaddy?"

"Y'all had better stay in here by the fire. It's mighty cold outside. I'll be right back."

When Granddaddy came back in the house, he'd always say, "I was on my way back from the barn while ago, and I heard something that sounded like bells a-tinkling, way back off yonder in the woods. I just can't figure why bells would be ringing back in the woods this time of the night."

"It's Santa Claus! It's Santa Claus!"

"Well, now, I never thought of that. I wonder if it was old Sandy Claws. You children had better get to bed. You know he won't come to see you as long as you're awake."

Then it was time to say good night. All the grandchildren would go around hugging all the grown-ups. "Good night Grandma, good night Granddaddy, good night Uncle Clyde, good night Aunt Mollie," and so forth.

We would always try to stay awake, lying on our pallets until Santa Claus got there, but we always lost the battle.

It sounded like the Third World War at Grandma's house on Christmas morning. There was cap pistols going off and baby dolls crying, and all the children hollering at the top of their lungs.

By the time the next school year started, I was six years old and in the first grade. I kept thinking about what Buford had said. I didn't want to believe it, but it kept slipping into the back door of my mind.

At school, Buford was three grades ahead of me, but I'd still see him sometimes. Every time he'd see me that whole year, he'd make it a point to rub it in about Santa Claus.

He'd do something like get me around a bunch of his older buddies and say, "Hey, you fellers, Curtis still believes in Santa Claus." And they'd all laugh and point.

Away from any adult persuasion, I guess Buford finally wore me out. I returned to Grandma's house the next year not believing that there was a Santa Claus. Christmas lost a little of its mystique. Oh, I still enjoyed it. I even pretended that I believed in "Sandy Claws" for Granddaddy's benefit, but it wasn't the same.

Well, as you know, time marches on, children grow up and leave home, including me.

I was living in Denver, Colorado, married, with a child, and I hadn't been home for Christmas since our little daughter had been born. Dawn was three that year, and this would be the first time that she really knew about Santa Claus, and she was some kind of excited.

We had the best time shopping for her, buying all the little toys that she wanted.

Daddy called me about three weeks before Christmas and said, "Son, you know that your grandparents are getting old. They've requested that all the children, grandchildren and great-grandchildren come home and spend Christmas with them at their house, the way we used to. Can you make it, son?"

"We'll be there, Daddy."

I couldn't think of a better place in the whole world for little Dawn to spend her first real Christmas, so we packed up and headed for North Carolina.

Grandma was eighty-two years old, but she still cooked all day long, and she still enjoyed every minute of it. Granddaddy was eighty-four, but he still had a twinkle in his eye and a mare in the barn.

The old house was fuller than ever, with a whole new generation of children in it. Everybody was there. Even Buford. He had married, but he didn't have any children. He didn't want any. One of my cousins said he figured Buford was too stingy to have children.

Buford was still the same, except that he had changed from a boy with a mean nature to a full-grown man with a cynical nature and a know-it-all attitude.

Just before we went into the front room for family prayer and the reading of the Christmas story, I overheard him say to somebody, "I don't know why Granddaddy keeps filling the children's heads full of that Santa Claus nonsense. I think it's ridiculous. If I had children, I wouldn't let him tell them all that junk."

I looked hard at Buford. I had never liked him, and I liked him even less now.

Our little daughter was so excited when Granddaddy started talking about "Sandy Claws" that she jumped up and down and clapped her hands.

When I took her up to bed, there was pure excitement in those big brown eyes. "Santa Claus coming, Daddy! Santa Claus coming, Daddy!"

I got a warm feeling all over, and I sure was glad to be back at Grandma's house at Christmas time.

After all the children had gone to sleep, the grown-ups started going out to their cars to get the toys they had brought for Santa Claus to leave under the Christmas tree.

I decided to wait until everybody else had finished before I put Dawn's presents out. This was a special time for me and I wanted to enjoy it.

After everybody had gone up to bed, I went out to the car to get Dawn's toys. To my shock, I couldn't find them. I ran back into the house to my wife. "Sylvia, where did you pack Dawn's Christmas presents?"

"I thought you packed them."

I was close to panic, but I didn't want Sylvia to know it. I said, "Oh well, you just go on to bed, honey, and I'll look again. I probably just overlooked them."

I kissed my wife good night and went back downstairs.

I knew I hadn't overlooked them. We had somehow forgot to pack them, and they were two thousand miles away in Denver, Colorado.

I was a miserable man. I just didn't feel like I could face little Dawn the next morning. She'd be so disappointed. All the other children would have the toys that Santa Claus had brought them, and my beloved little daughter wouldn't have anything.

How could I have been so dumb? Here it was, twelve o'clock Christmas Eve night, all the stores closed, everybody in bed, and me without a single present for little Dawn. I was heartbroken. I went into the front room and sat by the dying fire, dejected and hopeless.

I don't know how long I sat there staring at the embers, but sometime later on I heard a rustle behind me and somebody said, "You got a match, son?"

I turned around and almost fell on the floor. Standing not ten feet from me was a short, fat little man in a red suit, with a long white beard and a pipe sticking out of his mouth.

I couldn't move, I couldn't speak. He looked at me and chuckled.

"Have you got a match, son? I ran out and I want to get this pipe going."

When I finally got my voice back, all I could say was, "Who are you?"

"Well, people call me by different names in different parts of the world, but around here they call me Santa Claus."

"No, I mean who are you really?"

"I just told you, son. How about that match?"

I stumbled to the mantelpiece, got a kitchen match and gave it to him.

"Much obliged." He stood there lighting his pipe, with me looking at him like he was a ghost or something.

"How did you get in here?"

"Oh, I've got my ways."

"I thought you were supposed to slide down the chimney."

"That's a common misconception. Would you slide down a chimney with a fire at the bottom?"

"Well, no. I mean, no, sir."

"Well, neither would I."

"How did you get here?"

"I've got a sturdy sleigh and the finest team of reindeer a man could have."

"But we ain't got no snow."

Santa Claus laughed so hard that his considerable belly shook. "I don't need snow. Half the places I go in the world don't have snow. Besides, I like to get out of the snow once in a while. We have it year-round at the North Pole, you know."

"You mean you really live at the North Pole?"

"Of course, I've always lived at the North Pole. Don't you know anything about Santa Claus, son?"

"Well, yeah, but I thought it was all a big put-on for the children."

"That's the trouble with you grown-ups. You think that everything you can't see is a put-on. It's a shame grown people can't be more like children. They don't have any trouble believing in me."

"You mean you've really got a sleigh, with reindeer

named Donner and Blitzen and stuff like that?"

"That's right, son. There's Comet and Cupid and Donner and Blitzen and Dasher and Dancer and Prancer and Vixen. Of course, there's no Rudolph with the red nose. I don't know who came up with that one. Rudolph really is a put-on."

"But what are you doing here? Why did you come?"

"Because there's a little girl in this house who believes in me very much. Now, she'd be mighty disappointed to wake up Christmas morning and have nothing under the tree."

"You mean you came all the way here just because one little girl believes in you?"

"That's right, son. There's magic in believing. Besides, she's not the only one in this house who believes in me."

"Who else?"

"Why, your grandfather, of course."

"You mean Granddaddy wasn't putting us on all those years? He really believed in you?"

"Of course he believed in me."

"Well, why do you do this?"

"It's my way of celebrating the most important birthday in the history of man. Our Lord has given us so much. How can we do less?"

Santa Claus consulted a piece of paper he pulled out of his pocket and started taking a doll and other toys out of a big bag he had brought with him.

"Well, I've got to go, son. I've got a lot of stops to make before sunup. It's been real nice talking to you. Thanks for the match."

"Can I help you with your bag, Santa Claus?"

"No, that's all right, son. I'm used to carrying it."

I walked outside with him. "Where's your sleigh, Santa Claus?"

"It's parked right over there in the edge of the woods. You can come over and see it if you like."

I started walking over to his sleigh with him, but then I had a thought.

"I'm gonna have to miss seeing your sleigh and reindeer. Thank you so very much. You saved my life. God bless you, Santa Claus. I'll see you next year."

"God bless you, too, son, and a Merry Christmas to you and yours."

Santa Claus started across the yard toward his sleigh, and I went running back in the house like a wild man. I raced up the stairs. "Buford, Buford, get up!"

"What's the matter, is the house on fire?"

"No, but hurry. Come out on the upstairs porch."

Buford grumbled as he got up and followed me out on the upstairs porch.

"What in the heck do you want? It's cold out here."

"Just hush up and listen."

Well, we listened for a full minute and nothing happened.

"You're crazy. I'm going back to bed."

"Buford, if you go back in the house, you're gonna miss something that I want you, above all people, to see."

We waited for a little while longer and I had almost given up hope when I heard it. It was just a little tinkle at first, hanging on the frosty air and getting louder by the second. It was sleigh bells!

Buford looked at me and said, "Curtis, is this some kind of a joke or something?"

"No, Buford, I swear it ain't. Just wait a minute now!"

Charlie Daniels

The sound of sleigh bells was getting louder and Buford's face was getting whiter. "You got somebody out there doing that, ain't you? Admit it! You got somebody out there, ain't you?"

I didn't say a word. All of a sudden it sounded like somebody had flushed a covey of quail. That sleigh came up out of the woods and headed west, hovering just above the treetops.

Buford was speechless. I thought he was gonna pass out. He held on to the banister and took deep breaths.

Even if you believe so far, I know you ain't gonna believe this next part, but it really happened. Santa Claus made a big circle and turned and flew right around the house. I bet he won't over twenty feet from the upstairs porch when he passed by me and Buford. Old Santa Claus could really handle them reindeer. Then he headed west again, moving at a pretty good clip this time.

I hate to even tell you this next part, cause you'll think I took it right out of the book, but I didn't. Anyway, just about the time he was getting out of our hearing, he hollered, "Merry Christmas, everybody!"

And then he was gone.

"Curtis, do you know where Granddaddy keeps that bottle hid in the barn? I need me a drink."

I don't believe that Buford ever told anybody about seeing Santa Claus. I know I didn't, not until now. But I just had to tell somebody about it. It's been hard keeping it to myself all these years.

I'm a granddaddy myself now. That little girl that caused all this to happen with her faith in Santa Claus is grown and married and has a three-year-old girl and five-year-old boy.

Me and Sylvia moved back to North Carolina many years ago and bought a big old farmhouse. Now my grandchildren come and spend Christmas with me and their grandmother. There's not as many of us as there was at Grandma's house, but we have just as big a time and celebrate Christmas just as hard.

In fact, Christmas is about the only time of the year I'll take a drink. I always get me a pint of Old Granddad at Christmas time. Since the grandchildren are so small, I don't like to drink in front of them, so I keep my drinking whiskey hid out in the barn. When I want to go out there and get me a snort, I always tell the grandchildren that I've got to go see if the cows got corn.

Of course, all the grown-ups know why I'm going out to the barn, or at least they think they do.

I always make my last trip to the barn after I've read the Christmas story and had family prayer. Everybody thinks I'm going out to get me a snort, but they're wrong.

I'm just going out to hear the sleigh bells ring.

Me and Deke

ME AND DEKE Bonner was riding the grub line. Now, it wasn't because we was lazy. Hell, we'd a-been glad to work for any man who paid cowboy's wages. It was just that after the beef was rounded up and sold, the ranchers didn't need but a few hands to get them through till branding time.

It was a way of life to a cowhand. We'd done it before, and we'd probably do it again.

I mean, it won't all that bad, cause western folks are mighty generous. You could get a meal at any bunkhouse or any campfire, and they didn't belittle or low-rate a man for being down on his luck. It's just that a man likes to pull his own weight and have a little jingle in his jeans.

Anyway, me and Deke was riding the grub line and looking for work. Not just any kind of work, but cowboy work. We didn't mind doing anything as long as it could be done from horseback.

Now, don't get me wrong. Me and Deke had done our

Charlie Daniels

share of chopping wood and pitching hay and such. But if a man ever starts making his living punching cows, it seems like he's got this thing down inside of him that just won't let him be happy doing anything else.

You see, a cowboy's got his pride. To tell the truth, that's about all he's got. Now, you take me: I had a saddle, two pairs of socks, an extra shirt, a pair of boots (down at the heel), a slicker, a rope and a bay gelding with a little bit of age on him, but a damn good horse.

Deke was in about the same shape as me, except he didn't have but one pair of socks.

Anyway, we picked up two days of work outside Waco, working the cutting pens for a cow and calf outfit. We made three dollars apiece and headed west. But there just won't nothing happening. Everybody had all the help they needed, and the pickings were mighty slim. We was down to a can of tomatoes and a dime.

About forty miles east of El Paso, we run into this feller, all by his lonesome, that looked like he was in about the same shape as we was.

Now, folks tend to be a little suspicious of other folks they meet out in the middle of nowhere, so we kinda eyed this hombre real hard, and he did us, but after a while we got real friendly.

"You fellers looking for work?" he asked.

"We damn sure are. Do you know of anybody hereabouts hiring?"

"Nope, not really. But there's a feller that wants a hand to play nursemaid to a couple of bulls and take 'em back east. I was gonna sign on myself, but I'm on parole and can't leave the state."

"What might this feller's name be, and where do you

206

reckon we could find him at?"

"His name is Mr. Amos Ketchum, and you could probably find him at the Ketchum Land and Cattle Company in El Paso. He owns it."

Well, me and Deke thanked the gent and lit out for El Paso. We got there about ten o'clock in the morning, and we didn't have a bit of trouble finding this feller Ketchum. Seeing him was another story.

First they said he won't there. Then they said that the job was filled. Then they told us to get out.

Me and Deke was mighty disappointed and was just about to walk out the door when a commotion started inside Mr. Ketchum's office. We heard somebody holler, "Get out of my office, you son of a bitch," and then the door opened and out pops this big, tough-looking cowpoke. And then this little man come up behind him and kicked him right in the seat of the pants. And that big rascal didn't even look around.

"If I ever see you in El Paso again, you'd better bring you a preacher, because there's going to be a funeral. You got that, you obnoxious, cattle-rustling son of a bitch?"

"Yes, sir, Mr. Ketchum."

Well, me and Deke was flabbergasted to hear that little feller talk to that big feller that way, and kick him and all.

And then we seen the reason why walk out the door. He wasn't no big man but he was fancy dressed, and he had a great big diamond ring on one finger and wore a Colt .44 tied down tight.

I've seen a fair amount of gunfighters in my time. There's a difference between a punk kid tying on a gun and trying to make a reputation and a seasoned, cold-eyed, hard-ass, professional gunfighter. Well, this feller was in the latter class.

About the time that big old whipped puppy cowhand hit the door, Mr. Ketchum noticed me and Deke and hollered, "What in the hell do you two bums want?"

Well, Deke never was as bashful as I am, so he upped and said, "We heard that you might be looking for a couple a good bull nurses."

"Two good bull nurses, two good bull nurses. Hell, I can't even find *one* good bull nurse. What makes you think that I'd give you the job?"

I was really proud of old Deke. He stepped right up and said, "Because we're the two best men you can find for the job."

"Did you ever rustle any cattle? You'd better not lie to me, boy."

"No, sir, we ain't never rustled one single head."

"Do you have any warrants or paroles hanging over your head?"

"No, sir."

"Well, come on in for a minute, and we'll talk about it a little more." We followed him and that quick draw artist into his office.

Mr. Ketchum said, "What do you know about bulls, boy?"

"A little bit short of everything there is to know about 'em. What do you want to know?" said Deke.

"Don't get smart with Mr. Ketchum, cowboy," Blackie said. (I figured the gunfighter's name had to be Blackie because everything he wore was black. But I found out later that his real name was Chester Penrose.)

"No, sir, I sure won't trying to be smart. The man asked me a question and I answered him just as plain as I could."

Well, you could see that Mr. Ketchum liked old Deke, talking up that way.

"Where have you worked?"

"Well, for one, I've worked for the Oxbow. That's a bull outfit."

"And a damn good one," Mr. Ketchum said, "Chester, I think we might have our man."

"Mr Ketchum," Deke said right off, "I can't hire on if you can't take both of us."

"But it's a one-man job, boy. If you pull it off, you could end up a month from now with four hundred dollars."

"I'm sorry, Mr. Ketchum, but I can't hire on without my partner."

Mr. Ketchum thought for a minute and then said, "Well, I don't care if the two of you go, but you'll have to split the four hundred dollars."

Well, hell, I reckon we would split four hundred dollars. I never had two hundred dollars at one time in my whole life, and neither had Deke.

"What do you want us to do?" Deke asked.

"Well, it's really very simple. I just want to move two bulls to the east coast, and I want somebody to go along and make sure they get there in good health."

I hadn't said nothing through this whole thing, but I upped and said, "That would take two years driving them bulls to the east coast. And how would we get across the Mississippi River? I've heard tell that thing is ten miles wide and full of quicksand."

Mr. Ketchum and Chester Penrose looked at me with something akin to absolute disgust, and I was wishing that I'd a-kept my trap shut. Anyway I can't remember exactly how Mr. Ketchum said it, but it was something like this:

Charlie Daniels

He had two prize Santa Gertrudis bulls that had come off the King Ranch. He was sending them to New York City, New York, and some feller from somewhere on the other side of the Atlantic Ocean was sending him two bulls from over there to be picked up in New York City and brought back to El Paso.

Now, this is the part that got my old dander up. Mr. Ketchum had jumped out and built a customized railroad car with two pens for the bulls, living quarters for one man (but two men could squeeze in), all the hay and feed for the bulls, and a wood cookstove and plenty of chuck for the man. I mean men — me and Deke.

And he said that he'd lay in extra grub, but there was to be no drinking, no card playing, no smoking (cause we were liable to set them bulls on fire), and no fighting. He said that if we got them bulls to New York City in good shape that we'd get two hundred dollars (a hundred a piece), and that if we got them foreign bulls (he called 'em Brahmas) back to El Paso in one piece, we'd get another two hundred.

Well, me and Deke would a-shaved a grizzly bear's ass for two hundred dollars. We said, "When do you want us to leave?"

It was the next morning at six o'clock.

Me and Deke was fixing to walk out the door when Mr. Ketchum said, "You boys look like you could use a square meal. Give them an advance, Chester. You boys be at the depot at four o'clock in the morning," and he walked out of the room.

Well, this Chester Penrose give us a ten-dollar bill apiece and said, "If them bulls don't get delivered on both ends, Mr. Ketchum ain't gonna like it. And worse, I ain't

210

gonna like it." And he walked out the door.

Me and Deke decided that since we was gonna eat free for the next month, and that we was gonna make two hundred dollars in a month's time, that we owed it to ourselves to go out and have us a fling.

So we parked our horses at the livery stable and went and eat a steak as big as a horse's lip from his eye down. From there we headed on down to the border and over into Juarez, where we proceeded to raise hell all night. We drank enough tequila to drown a good size heifer yearling, and we was a sorry-looking bunch when we got to the depot at four o'clock.

Mr. Ketchum and Chester Penrose and a couple of hands was already there with a pair of the best-looking Santa Gertrudis bulls that me and Deke had ever seen. They loaded them big rascals just as simple as pie.

Me and Deke pulled our hats down low over our faces and tried not to breathe in Mr. Ketchum's face. We got mighty busy getting up in the car and making sure everything was right for the bulls. I figure he knew we'd been drinking, but he didn't say anything about it. In fact, he didn't say a damn word the whole time. Neither did that cold-eyed devil, Chester Penrose, which suited me and Deke just fine.

We slipped one of them cowhands off to the side and asked him, "How we gonna know when we get to New York City, New York? We ain't been no further east than Fort Worth."

"Just stay on the train. That's where they drop the car off. You boys better go easy on that drinking. Mr. Ketchum frowns on it."

"Thanks for the advice, partner," we said.

Charlie Daniels

You ought to a-seen that little bunkhouse they had built in that car. I mean, it was something. It had a bed (me and Deke decided we'd swap off sleeping in it), a cookstove and all kinds a grub, and a waterbarrel. Me and Deke hadn't never seen nothing like it.

And them bulls had it made, too. There was two big pens that were padded all over, with built-in feed and water troughs and a window that slid back in the side of the car where them bulls could see the country as they was riding up to New York City, New York.

Oh, it was a fancy rig all right, and we was mighty glad about signing on with Mr. Ketchum. It looked like an easy way to make four hundred dollars.

That old train was five minutes early, and by a quarter past six we was rolling east and it was almost good daylight.

Me and Deke learned a long time ago not to get attached to any horse. Horses in cattle country might not be around too long. But a good saddle was another thing, and that was all we brought aboard, and I took the first turn on the floor and used mine for a pillow.

We woke up a few hours later and the train had stopped to take on water. We got up and fed the bulls, or I fed the bulls and Deke rustled up a mess of bacon and cooked some biscuits. We ate and looked out the window, but Texas all looks the same out west, so after awhile we kinda looked at one another, and I think we had the same thing on our minds.

You see, when I said that all me and Deke brought was our saddles, I told a little fib. Lashed under our saddles we had three bottles of tequila apiece. Me and Deke figured that it would be good to have it along for medicinal purposes.

Anyway, I said, "Now, Deke, you know Mr. Ketchum said we couldn't be drinking none."

Deke said, "Now, pard, he was just talking about when we was on duty. Them bulls don't need both of us to watch them, so one of us will watch the bulls and one of us will drink."

"Well, which one is gonna watch and which one is gonna drink?"

"We'll flip a coin."

"Deke, you know we ain't got no coin. We spent every last cent we had."

Well, Deke studied on it for awhile, and then he said, "If them bulls is facing in the same direction, you get to drink. If they ain't, then I get to drink." Well, wouldn't you know it, them bulls was turned opposite of one another. So I started watching and Deke started drinking.

After about an hour, Deke said, "Now, I'll watch for an hour and you can drink."

I said, "But Deke, you can't be on duty drinking."

"I ain't gonna be drinking. I'm all through drinking for an hour, so I won't be drinking on duty."

Well, it made perfectly good sense to me. So me and Deke switched places and I drank for an hour. We watched them bulls all night, but neither one of us took a single drink on duty.

The next day we stopped at a water tank, and me and Deke shoveled out the bulls' pens and put fresh water in the troughs. Then we walked around a little bit and went in and laid down.

Well, sir, a few days later we was in country like me and Deke hadn't never seen before. Water everywhere, creeks and rivers and lakes, and we seen more trees in one day than we had in our whole life put together.

I was a little disappointed in the Mississippi River, though. It won't no ten miles wide. Now, don't get me wrong; it was the biggest damn river me and Deke had ever seen, but it won't no ten miles wide.

I couldn't begin to tell you all the things that me and Deke seen, but it was considerable. And the first thing we knew, we was in New York City, New York.

Them bulls was in just as good a shape as they were when we left Texas, and just like clockwork this feller met us and took the bulls and give us two hundred dollars. He even give us another forty to buy grub with for the trip back.

But them foreign bulls was gonna be a couple of days late, he said, so me and Deke was gonna be in New York City, New York, for three days. We decided that we'd get a hotel room and whoop it up a little bit.

We asked this feller how people got around in New York City, New York, and he told us about these buggies that they had to hire out. He called 'em hacks. Them hacks was the fanciest-looking buggies you ever laid eyes on.

Well, me and Deke got us one and told him to take us to the hotel. He asked us something. I couldn't understand nothing nobody said, they all talked so funny, but Deke figured out that he said, "What hotel?"

Deke told him that we didn't care which hotel, but to damn well get us to some hotel pronto. The feller driving that hack got kinda sassy, and Deke told him if he didn't take us to the hotel, that he was gonna jerk a knot in his ass. The feller said something that me nor Deke neither one didn't understand and took off kinda huffylike.

We rode and we rode, and I never knew that there were so many houses in the world. And great big, tall buildings. I got scared thinking about one a them big, tall buildings falling on us, but Deke said it won't likely, and other than that I enjoyed the ride.

About that time the hack stopped in front of this place called the Delmonico Hotel. Deke paid that hack feller and almost got into it again. The rascal wanted to charge us a dollar for a three-mile buggy ride. I told Deke to go ahead and pay the dollar. Hell, we had plenty of money, and we didn't want to cause no trouble in New York City, New York.

Well, Deke give him the dollar, and I'll be damned if that feller didn't cuss at Deke when he took off down the street. Deke chased him for awhile, but that feller whipped up his horse and Deke give it up.

We shouldered our saddles and headed for the door.

That's when we met Armand. Armand was the politest little feller you ever seen. He was dressed in this green suit with brass buttons, and he had a job standing out in the street in front of the Delmonico Hotel.

Anyway, Armand said, "I'm sorry, gentlemen, but you can't enter. We have certain dress codes which must be observed."

I figured Deke was gonna punch him, but like I said, Armand was such a nice little feller that Deke liked him right off.

Deke said, "You know, pard, me and you could do with a haircut and a shave and a bath. It wouldn't even hurt for us to get us a change of clothes."

Armand piped right up and said, "Gentlemen, there's a barbershop on the corner with bathing facilities and a

215

haberdasher's right next door. I'm sure they'd be honored
to serve you."

Me and Deke made a deal with Armand to watch our
saddles for awhile, and we moseyed on down the street.

Well, buddy, me and Deke got the whole nine yards. I
mean, a bath, a shave and a haircut, and then we bought us
each a suit and a walking cane and one of them derby hats.
We was hot stuff. We was dressed up fit to kill.

We went back down to the Delmonico Hotel, and I mean
to tell you we looked as good as anybody. I wish you
coulda seen me and Deke.

Deke said, "Pard, before we sign into the hotel, let's get
us something to eat. I'm hungry."

I was ready to tie on the feedbag myself, so we went
looking for the dining room. When we got there, this feller
met us at the door and asked if we had some reservations.
Deke told him no, and that feller made us wait for a half
hour before he gave us a table to eat at.

I never seen a place so fancy in all my life. Everything
was silver and linen, and the waiters was all dressed up and
didn't wear aprons or anything. I mean, it was first class.

This feller come and jerked our napkins off a the table
and put them on our knees, and said, "Good evening.
Would you like a cocktail before dinner?"

"A what?" Deke asked him.

"A drink, gentlemen. Would you care for a drink before
dinner?"

Deke said, "Hell, yeah, bring us one."

Well, the feller just kept standing there looking at us,
and after a little bit Deke says, "Pardner, I thought you was
gonna bring us a drink."

The feller kinda pushed his lips together and said, "Sir,

how can I bring you a drink when I don't know what you want to drink?"

"Oh, I'm sorry," Deke said real nicelike. "What do people drink around here?"

"They drink all kinds of things, sir. Please give me your drink order. I have another table waiting."

Deke said, "Bring me a drink of whiskey. How about you, pard?" And I nodded.

"Is that on ice or neat?"

"How about running that by me one more time, pardner."

"Do you want the whiskey on ice or straight? Please, sir, I'm in a hurry."

Deke looked at me and I just shook my head, and Deke said, "Well, just bring us the bottle."

"Sir, Delmonico's doesn't serve spirits by the bottle. Only champagne and table wine. Now, please, sir, I've got to be moving on. The headwaiter's looking at me."

"Well, just bring us a good straight drink apiece and another one right behind her."

"Very good, sir. What brand would you prefer?"

"Bring us Old Southern. How about you, pard?" I nodded.

"What, sir?"

"Old Southern."

"Very good, sir, thank you," and he took off like a scalded cat.

In about two minutes he was back. "Sir, the bartender says that we have no Old Southern, that he has never heard of Old Southern. Now, please, sir, give me your drink order. I'm going to lose my job."

I could see that Deke was getting hot under that new

collar. He said, "Now, listen to me, feller. If you'd a-done what I told you to start with and a brought us a drink of whiskey, you wouldn't be having all this big fuss. Now, bring us a drink of whiskey or forget it."

That feller took off like he was shot out of a gun and brought us two drinks of the best, I mean *the* best whiskey that I ever wet my beak in.

About as soon as we got through with that first one, we was ready for another one. But we didn't see our feller anywhere.

After awhile Deke said, "Hell, pard, I'll just walk over there and get 'em myself."

"I'll go with you, Deke," I said.

Well, me and Deke walked up to the bar and Deke hollered at the bartender, "Hey, pardner, give us about a water glass of that last stuff we just had."

I tell you, I didn't like that bartender right off. I mean, he looked at us like we was coyotes and said, "Please do not raise your voice in here, sir. This is a respectable establishment."

So Deke said just as nice as he could in a real low voice, "I said to give us about a water glass full of that last stuff we had."

"What stuff?"

"That stuff you just sent us."

"I don't know what you're talking about."

"You know, the whiskey you just sent over to us. We want some more of it."

"Sir, I have a restaurant full of customers. How could I possibly remember which drink I sent to which table?" And I could tell that he didn't like me and Deke one damn bit.

"I'm getting damn sick and tired of dealing with this rawhide outfit," Deke said. "Just give us a water glass full of your very best whiskey."

The bartender got all excited. "I'll give you anything you want, just please lower your voice."

"Is there a damn law against talking loud in this town?" And that's all Deke had to say on the subject.

"If you'll just please go back to your table, sir, I'll send it right over. Now, please go back to your table. Which table do you have?"

"The one between the big fat lady and the baldheaded man and them three tin-horn dudes with the slicked-back hair."

Me and Deke headed back to the table, and it won't long before that first feller come back and brought us about ten shot glasses full of whiskey.

Then another feller we hadn't seen before come up and handed us these menus that was wrote out on this fancy cardboard kinda stuff. He poured us a glass of water and started picking up the empty shot glasses off the table. He said, "Good evening, gentlemen. Our specialty this evening is *Coq au Vin*, served with sauteed mushrooms and French beans. I'll give you some time to consider the menu. I'll be back in a few minutes." And he was gone.

I said, "Deke, what did he say?"

"The only word I understood was beans, and I sure don't want to be eating any beans. Hell, I eat 'em everyday. I want me a great big steak and a bate of apple pie."

Then we got to looking at them menus. Now, me and Deke both read some, but neither one of us could buck out that menu. So we just shut 'em up and laid 'em on the table.

219

When the waiter came back, Deke says, "We both want a steak, the biggest ones you got."

The feller wrote something down in his tallybook. He said, "And how do you gentlemen like your steaks?"

"We like 'em real good," said Deke.

"But, sir, how do you wish it served?"

"Well, on a plate, if you've got one."

"But, sir, how do you want it cooked?"

"On a stove or whatever you got back there. What kind of damn fool question is that anyway?"

"But, sir, do you want it rare, medium rare, medium done or well done. We don't recommend the well done."

"Well, bring it to us the first way you said."

"Very good, sir, and what vegetables will you be having this evening? We have the cauliflower *au gratin*, the French-cut string beans, the sauteed mushrooms and the *pommes frites*."

It all sounded like something they threw out of the chuck wagon.

Deke said, "Just bring us the two steaks and some bread."

"And dessert?"

Deke didn't even hesitate this time. He said, "Apple pie. I think we can handle a whole one tonight, don't you, pard?" And I nodded yes.

That waiter looked like somebody had pulled his tail, but he kept on writing in his tallybook.

"Would you gentlemen care to split a Caesar salad?"

"Why not? Bring us one of 'em."

"Will you be having wine with your dinner?"

"I hadn't thought about it. What do you think pard?"

"I ain't never done it before, Deke."

"I ain't neither, so let's give her a try. Yeah, bring us some."

"May I recommend a Chateau Margot Sauvignon?"

"A what?"

"A very good bottle of wine, sir."

"Well, that's what we want, a very good bottle of wine. Bring it on."

We was sitting there talking when this feller come up pushing this little cart with a great big bowl full of rabbit food and all these little bottles and things setting on it.

He commenced to mixing up that rabbit food with all kinds of stuff. A little bit of this and a little bit of that, and I was looking forward to tasting it till he broke a raw egg in it. I mean raw, just like it come out of the hen.

When he got done mixing it all up, he dished it up into two bowls and set them in front of me and Deke. Deke had a bit of his, but I never did touch mine. I just ain't gonna eat no raw egg.

I said, "Deke, I hope this ain't the best they can do."

Deke said, "Yeah, pard, whoever runs this outfit has got an awful lot of tightening up to do."

We was getting mighty hungry when they brought them steaks out, but when I cut into mine, blood popped out of it. I thought I was gonna upchuck right on the floor. I mean, I seen a lot of blood in my life in a lot of places, but I ain't never seen blood come out of something on somebody's plate.

Deke was getting upset, too. "These things is raw."

"You ordered them rare, sir," said that waiter feller.

"I didn't order no raw steaks. Now, take them son of a bitches back to the kitchen and tell Cookie to cook it till it's done. You got that?"

He jerked them steaks up pronto and lit out for the kitchen. In a few minutes, he was back with 'em cooked right.

Then a feller brought this wine and opened it up and smelled the cork and poured a little bit in this tiny pan that he wore about his neck. He swished it around in his mouth, swallowed it and made a face, and then smiled and kinda bowed and poured a little bit of it in Deke's glass. Then he just stood there.

Deke said, "Pour one for my pard, too, and while you're at it, pour me a little more."

Deke claimed that he liked it; I thought it was the worst-tasting mess I ever tried to drink. But them steaks was mighty good after they got 'em cooked right. So me and Deke ordered another one apiece and told that feller to bring us our apple pie while we waited.

I'll say one thing. That apple pie was as good as any me and Deke had ever had. We eat two of 'em and got one to carry with us.

When we were done eating our steaks, the feller brought out some cups and poured us some coffee, and me and Deke was full as ticks. I kinda sat back in my chair and looked around a little bit and thought my eyes was playing tricks on me. I said, "Deke, you see that big-nosed feller over there with that real homely looking, gray-headed woman?"

"Yeah."

"Well, tell me, what is that on his plate?"

Deke looked over that way for a long time, and then he said, "Damn, pard, that looks like snails."

"That's what I thought."

"Is he eating 'em?"

"Hell, yeah, he's eating 'em."

Me and Deke sat there and studied for a minute, and Deke said, "I bet I know what it is. He don't know he's eating snails. He thinks they're something else. These folks up here probably don't even know what a snail looks like. Hell, they might not even have snails in New York City, New York."

"Somebody ought to tell him, Deke."

"Yeah, I reckon somebody ought to tell him." And Deke got up and went over to their table.

"Excuse me, mister."

"Yes, what is it?"

"Do you know what you're eating?"

"Of course, I know what I'm eating. I'm eating escargot."

"No, sir. I hate to be the one to tell you this, but you're eating snails."

"I know."

"You know?"

"Of course, I know, and what business is it of yours?"

"Did you know that snails crawl on the ground, and they're all slimy and they leave this little trail of gloppy stuff behind them, and they have these two little horn kinda things on their head?"

That feller slung his fork down on the table and said, "You ruined my dinner, you uncouth imbecile."

"Now, feller, don't get so all-fired huffy. I was trying to do you a good turn. I don't give a damn — excuse me, ma'am — if you eat worms and buzzard guts." And Deke come back and sat down.

I don't believe that feller eat another bite, and pretty soon they got up and left in a huff.

"These is funny people up here, Deke. You can't hardly

understand them talk, they eat snails, and they get riled if you try to do them a favor. I'll be glad to get back to Texas."

"Me, too, pard. Let's go pay up and get out of here." Deke stood up and put a chew of tobacco in his mouth, and I did likewise. Now, me and Deke ain't the kind of fellers to chew tobacco on the inside, in the company of ladies, but we was leaving and we figured we wouldn't have to spit till we got outside.

About the time we stood up, though, this feller come running up and said, "You can't leave without the check. You must pay the bill. Wait and I will bring it to you." And he went sashaying off.

Well, we waited and we waited, and I was just about to drown. I said, "Deke, I'm gonna have to spit."

Deke said, "Try to hold her a minute, pard, there's ladies in here."

In a few minutes, I said, "Deke, I'm gonna have to spit, ladies or no ladies."

"Well, hold your head down low and try to spit in that coffee cup."

That worked pretty good, and I had that cup slam full by the time that feller come back with the bill.

I figured I'd put that cup under my coat and set it down at the front door or something. But when I stood up to get a headstart, I caught my foot on the chair leg and tripped and dumped that whole cup of tobacco juice in a bowl of some kind of soup the feller at the next table was eating.

You could hear the whole dining room buzzing, and people was getting up out of their chairs.

This feller in a black suit come running up and said, "Out! Out!"

"But we got to pay our bill," Deke said.

"It's on the house, don't worry about it. Just leave before you put me out of business."

I apologized to Deke when we got outside, but he just said, "Don't worry about it, pard. A little tobacco juice ain't never hurt nobody. I got an idea. Let's don't even stay here tonight. Let's go stay at the railroad yards."

I said I'd sure be proud to do that. And we went and seen Armand and got our saddles and Deke give him a dollar and said, "You're the only feller in this whole place that's got a damn lick of sense. Where can a feller get a decent drink of whiskey around here?"

Well, Armand said there was a place just a little ways down the street, so me and Deke shook hands with Armand and lit out.

We walked into that place, laid our saddles on the floor and leaned on the bar. This place would sell a feller a bottle, so we ordered one.

There was five or six fellers shooting pool in the back, and one of 'em walked up to where me and Deke was standing. "Hey, cowboys, where are your horses?"

"They're in El Paso, Texas, and we wish we was there with them."

"What's the matter, the big city treating you rough?"

"No, we ain't been in no fights or nothing, but these people up here sure are hard to figure out."

"Well, you've just been around the wrong people, that's all. Where you boys from?"

"West Texas."

"Well, I'm from Dallas myself. I know I don't sound like it, but I've been up here so long I talk just like these people. Come on back and meet my friends."

Charlie Daniels

He introduced me and Deke to a right friendly bunch of fellers, and we shot a couple of games of pool with them. Them fellers was all dressed up with gold watch chains and stuff, and they insisted on buying.

After awhile, Willie (that's the first feller we met), he said, "It's a pity that you boys don't have any money. We could let you in on something that could make you rich in about a week. It's just a real shame that you boys don't have any money."

I said, "Hell, we got two hundred dollars."

"That's strange," Willie said, "that's exactly how much we needed. Let me tell you about it. You see, when we first came up here, we bought a bridge that nobody wanted. Since that time things have built up around it so much that now everybody wants it. We charge a toll to everybody who comes across the bridge. Well, we've made so much money, and we miss Texas so much, that when we saw you come in and found out you were from Texas, we decided to let you have it for two hundred dollars. We'll just get on a train and go back to Texas. We don't need to make any more money. We've got enough to last us the rest of our lives."

Deke upped and said, "Well, if you don't need to make no more money, why don't you just give us the bridge?"

"It's against the law to do that in New York City. We'd like to give it to you, but the law says that when you get rid of a bridge, you've got to get at least two hundred dollars for it."

"Oh, I see. But we ain't gonna be in town long enough to run no bridge."

"You fellers could start early in the morning and by ten o'clock, you'd have your two hundred dollars back. Then you could sell it to somebody else for two hundred dollars and double your money. I'll guarantee it."

Deke said, "Well, how in the world would we make people know it was our bridge, with you fellers running it so long and all?"

"I've got the deed right here in my pocket. I could sign it over to you." And he pulled out a piece of paper with all kinds of writing and seals and stuff on it.

Well, me and Deke might just be cowhands, but we won't dumb. Nobody but a fool would turn down a deal like that.

Deke said, "Wait a minute. If we give you our whole two hundred dollars, we'll be stone broke and won't have no walking-around money to last till in the morning."

"Fellows, what do you say? They seem like real nice guys, so let's let them have it for a hundred and ninety. We'll just put two hundred on the deed, and the law will never know about it."

Well, I spoke up and said, "That's downright decent of you fellers."

"Think nothing of it," said Willie, and he pulled out a pen and some ink and signed the deed over to me and Deke.

We give him a hundred and ninety dollars and he said, "Congratulations, gentlemen, you now own the Brooklyn Bridge."

Me and Deke left soon after that so we could get up early and start getting rich. We caught us one of them hacks and went back to our railroad car and bedded down. It was awful hard to sleep for thinking about our new bridge.

"You know, Deke, I'll bet that after we get our two

hundred dollars back in the morning, that if we played our cards right, we could probably get four or five hundred dollars for that thing."

"I was thinking the same thing. Or, hell, we might just keep it and hire somebody to run it for us and send the money to us in Texas."

"That's a damn good idea, Deke. Good night."

"Night, pard."

We got up at four o'clock the next morning and it was raining. We had one hell of a time finding one of them hacks, and while we was riding over, Deke says, "You know, pard, I wonder if this rain will kinda slow things down over at the bridge today. It might take us till twelve or one o'clock to get our two hundred dollars back."

"You know, I was thinking, Deke, why don't we go ahead and run the bridge for the other two days we're gonna be here, and then we can just give the damn thing to some old boy. We don't live in New York City, New York. We ain't worried about what this law up here says. Shoot, we'll probably be gone before they even hear about it."

"Good thinking, pard, good thinking."

"Which end of the Brooklyn Bridge do you gentlemen want off on?" the driver asked.

"Drop him off at one end and me off at the other. You see, pard, that way we'll get 'em coming and going."

"Well, how much do you think we ought to charge?"

"How about a nickel?"

"Ain't that a little steep?"

"It's our damn bridge. If they don't want to pay a nickel, let the stingy son of a bitches swim. Of course, if you see some old boy that looks down on his luck or a lady with a bunch of kids, I say we ought to let them go across free. But everybody else pays, and I think it ought to be a nickel."

Well, a nickel it was.

Deke dropped me off at my end of the bridge and said, "When you get up to a hundred dollars, let me know," and he headed on down to his end.

It had quit raining and was almost daylight. The first thing to come across my end of the bridge was a fancy carriage, and he acted like he won't gonna stop. So I reached out and grabbed ahold of the horse's bridle.

The feller driving looked down at me and said, "What's the meaning of this?"

"We're the new owners, and I don't know what the old owners charged, but me and Deke is charging a nickel."

"Owners of what?"

"Of this here bridge, and you can either pay a nickel or you can swim across."

"I do believe you're serious."

About that time a head with a top hat came out the window and said, "What's the hold up, Robert? I've got to get home. Rachel is going to raise hell as it is."

"Some clowns out here trying to make us pay a toll to go across the Brooklyn Bridge, Mr. Carrington."

"Well, pay him and let's go."

"But Mr. Carrington."

"Pay him, Robert!"

"Yes, sir," and he flipped me a nickel and took off.

I said, "Thank you very much. We hope to be doing a lot of business with y'all. Don't mind that feller on the other end. He's just taking up from people coming from that-a-way. Good morning."

Hot damn, I was feeling good. All me and Deke had to

do was to stand here and make money. We was gonna be rich.

The next thing to come across my end of the bridge was one of them hacks, and when I finally got him pulled over, I said, "What the hell you trying to do, run me down? The new toll's a nickel."

"What?"

"I said cough up a nickel, dude, if you want to go across my bridge."

"Your bridge?"

"Mine and Deke's."

"Screw you, you crazy son of a bitch. You can't own the Brooklyn Bridge. Get the hell out of the way."

"Let me tell you something, you little goggle-eyed weasel. I ain't gonna be too many more of them son of a bitches! Now, give me a nickel or get the hell off my bridge."

You could tell that it just galled him, but he give me a nickel and hit his horse real hard with his whip and just went shooting off.

The next feller that come across was walking and looked a little bit on the shabby side, so I decided to let him slide. I said, "Good morning, pardner. I'm gonna let you across free this morning." Do you know that feller didn't even thank me for letting him across free? He just looked at me and kept on walking.

The next people to come across was two fellers walking. They looked pretty prosperous, so I said, "Good morning, boys. That'll be a nickel apiece."

"A nickel apiece for what?"

"That's what the new toll is. We just took over this morning."

"You're crazy."

"Listen, feller, I done been called a son of a bitch this morning, and I'm getting tired of people insulting me. So give me a nickel or you ain't coming across our bridge."

"Get out of the way," said one, and they started walking toward me.

Well, I reached out and grabbed the biggest one by the arm and twisted it up behind his back.

"That hurts. Stop!"

"I'll break the damn thing off if you don't give me a nickel apiece."

"Pay him, Harold. He's a crazy man! Oh, I'm sorry; you're not crazy."

Well, Harold give me a dime and I turned him aloose. I said, "The next time I ain't gonna take the time to be nice. Look, I done lost two buggies and a hack fooling around with y'all!"

Things were picking up. There was all kinds of buggies and carriages and hacks out, and it looked like a lot of 'em were heading our way. I stepped out in the traffic and stopped a carriage and said, "Good morning, that'll be five cents, please."

That driver was downright insulting. "Get out of the way, you fool. You're holding up the mayor of New York City. How dare you stop this carriage, you idiot."

I said, "Feller, that done it. If you'd a-come up here acting halfway decent and said you had the mayor of New York City, New York, with you, I'd a-let you go across free. But since you've got to be such a hard-headed peckerwood, I'll just charge you double. Now, it'll cost you a dime. Like Deke says, it's our bridge."

He tried to whip his horses and go right over the top of

me, but I can hold horses all day long if I can get in front of 'em and get me a hold. Them horses won't going nowhere.

Well, the door of that carriage opened and out stepped the biggest man I've ever seen. He come around to the front of the rig and said, "What's the trouble, Jim?"

"That fool won't turn loose of the horses. Something about a toll."

That big feller walked up to me and said, "Look, buddy, I'm the mayor's bodyguard, and if you don't turn loose of those horses, I'm gonna have to hurt you bad."

"I can't."

"Why?"

"I said I wouldn't and I can't go back on my word."

I could see that he figured that he was going to enjoy this. I knew damn well I won't going to, but a feller's got to protect his property, so I stood my ground.

He come at me and I whopped him across the nose with my walking cane. My cane broke and so did his nose, and he was so mad that he reminded me of an old longhorn bull I seen tear the wall out of a barn one time. I mean, he was hot! He come charging at me again.

I just kinda sidestepped him and stuck my foot out and tripped him as he went by, and he went down on his all fours and tore the knees out of his britches. But he kept getting up and I was running out of tricks.

He come tearing out at me again, and I got lucky that time because he slipped and busted his ass on that wet pavement. I got ahold of a barrel stave that was laying on the bridge, and when he got up, I wore him out with it.

He didn't get up that time, and right about then Deke come running up.

"What's the matter, pard? I could see you fighting as I was headed on down this way."

"These folks don't want to pay the toll because they're hauling the mayor of New York City, New York."

"Well, he ain't no better than anybody else. I ain't had nothing but trouble down at my end. I been jerking people around all morning, so I figured I'd come on down here and help you. We'll just work one end together till these people get used to paying the nickel."

"That sure suits me, Deke."

That big feller was getting up off of the ground, and I said, "Watch him, Deke." But you could tell he didn't want no more.

There was all kinds of buggies and carriages backed up on my side, and everybody that was coming across the other way was stopping to see what was going on. Everything had just come to a standstill.

Deke stepped up and hollered, "They ain't none of y'all going nowhere till this feller pays us."

There was people hollering and calling us names and carrying on, but me and Deke just stood our ground, and I still had a barrel stave in my hand. Well, it looked like a Mexican standoff for a few minutes.

Then somebody hollered, "Here comes the police," and about eight men in blue suits come running up.

One of 'em went up and opened the carriage door and said, "Are you all right, Your Honor? We came as quick as we could." And then they all walked up to where me and Deke was standing.

"Just what in the hell is going on? What happened to Tiny?"

"I had to bust him up a little bit cause he wouldn't pay

the toll."

"You whipped Tiny McCloskey? I'll say one thing for you, son, you're tough. Tiny McCloskey is the best street fighter I've ever seen, and I've been on the force for thirty years."

"What makes you think you can collect toll on the Brooklyn Bridge?" asked another one.

"Deke stepped up and said, "Because we own it. I got the deed to it right here." And he pulled the deed out of his pocket.

"You poor, naive fools. You didn't fall for that old gag. I feel sorry for you, but I'm gonna have to take you in anyway. You'll probably do time for this before the mayor gets through with you. Put the cuffs on 'em boys."

Well, I looked at Deke and Deke looked at me. It looked like the whole town was in front of us, but there won't nothing behind us but a clear open lane, and that's the way we went. I mean, we skedaddled.

Most of them police was real fat and couldn't run worth a durn. Me and Deke was flat moving out. We was way ahead of them fellers by the time we got across the bridge. Now, we didn't like running from the law, but we figured we hadn't done nothing wrong, and damned if we was gonna go to jail for it.

We'd done shook every one of them police. The only trouble was that we was as lost as a July snow. We didn't have no idea which way the railroad yards was.

Deke said, "You know, pard, I've been studying on it, and them railroad yards is on the other side of the river. We gonna have to figure out a way to get back across."

I said, "Deke, why don't we get us one of them hacks. Don't you reckon he'd know the way to the railroad yards?"

"Good thinking, pard."

So we found us a hack, and sure enough, he knew where the railroad yards was at and took us there. We couldn't tell the feller driving that we didn't want to go back across the bridge again, and when we did you better know that me and Deke got down mighty low in that hack. But all them police was gone and nobody didn't pay no particular attention to us.

We was feeling right good about getting away from them police and all, and after a while Deke said, "Pard, I sure could use a snort after all that. What do you say we stop and get one?"

I said, "Deke, I don't believe I've ever needed one no worse than I do right now. In fact, I might just have two."

We was almost back to the railroad yards, and Deke hollered and told that feller driving to drop us off at a saloon.

We went inside and was just having our third drink when the door opens and who walks in but Willie the Bridge Seller. He didn't notice us standing at the bar, and he sat down at a table and ordered a beer. There won't nobody in the place but the bartender and Willie and me and Deke.

We let old Willie get settled down real good, and then we walked up to his table. Deke said, "Hey, Willie, remember us?"

You could tell that Willie did remember us, and he tried to get up out of his chair, but I was standing behind him and pinned him.

Deke throttled him by the throat and said, "You polecat son of a lowdown bitch. You ain't no honest man. You got us in a scrape with the law. I don't believe you ever did own that bridge, and furthermore, I don't believe you're even from Texas."

Well, old Willie's eyes got as big as silver dollars, and he said, "Wait a minute, boys. I sold you that bridge fair and square, and a deal is a deal."

Deke said, "I'll tell you what the deal is, pardner. You're gonna give us our two hundred dollars back and we're gonna give you your deed back."

"I can't do that. I've already spent the money. I'll tell you what. If you don't like the bridge, I've got this building I can let you have for the same amount. I've got the deed right here in my pocket and I'll trade it to you for the bridge."

"We don't want your building or nothing else you got. We just want our money. Search him, pard."

I got busy searching Willie's pockets and come up with a wad of cash money that would choke a mule and counted off two hundred dollars.

"But you didn't give me but a hundred and ninety."

"The other ten's operating expenses."

I said, "Deke, didn't this feller guarantee us that we'd make at least two hundred dollars off a this deal? Don't you think we ought to take that, too?"

"Good thinking, pard, good thinking," and I counted off another two hundred.

Well, as it turned out, that bartender thought that me and Deke was robbing old Willie, and he snuck out the door and in a few minutes he was back with a police.

Me and Deke had had all the truck we wanted with the police for one day, so we took off out the back with Willie and that police hot in behind us.

Now, this police could run pretty good, and they fol-

lowed us right into the railroad yards. We hid behind a
boxcar and they went running right on by, and me and
Deke headed for that customized railroad car just as hard
as we could go.

"Let's get out of these suits, pard."

So we took off them fancy outfits and put on our old
clothes and got busy shoveling out them bull pens.

A few minutes later, Willie and that police came by.
"Have you seen two men running by here?" the police
asked.

"Nope," said Deke, and we kept right on shoveling.

"I'm sorry, mister, but it looks like they got away," the
police said, and him and Willie went walking off.

After they was gone, me and Deke had us a real good
belly laugh. We was two hundred dollars richer and still
had the deed to the Brooklyn Bridge. We laid in supplies
for the trip back and stayed in that railroad car till them
other two bulls got there.

I wish you coulda seen them bulls. They was great big
rascals. They was brindled-colored, and their old ears
hung down beside their heads. They had this big hump on
their withers, and they didn't like one another one bit.

We had a hell of a time getting them loaded, and even
after we got them in the pens, they kept snorting and
pawing at one another.

I said, "Deke, them things looks like trouble to me."

"Me, too, pard. We're gonna have to watch them boys
real close."

Me and Deke was some kind of glad to see that train pull
out of New York City, New York. We'd seen enough of
that place to last us the rest of our lives.

Now, me and Deke have seen some ornery bulls in our

time, but we hadn't never seen nothing like these two. I mean, they didn't let up. They was snorting and blowing and kicking and pawing and knocking around in them pens. You couldn't get close to them. The only way we could clean out the pens was to put a rope on their horns and tie them up snug to the side of the car. And even then they'd beller and paw and try to get at you.

I said, "Deke, if them son of a bitches belonged to me, I'd put a bullet right between their eyes. They're gonna tear this customized railroad car all to pieces before we get back to Texas."

I mean, they was keeping us up all night, trying to keep them from getting at one another. It was a long trip.

When we got to Kansas City, the train pulled into the stockyards to drop off some cars and left us setting on a sidetrack. There must a been five thousand cows in heat in them stockyards, the way them bulls acted. After a while, one of them calmed down a little bit, but the other one kept on butting the side of the car. Me and Deke figured we'd better put a rope on his horns and tie him off to keep him from hurting hisself.

Deke got the gate open and I tossed a houlihan around his horns, but before I could jerk my slack, he got out of it and headed for me and Deke, hellbent for leather. We jumped out of the way, and he went right out that open door and was gone, tearing ass right through the middle of the Kansas City stockyards.

Me and Deke was in a tither. Mr. Ketchum's prize bull was running loose a thousand miles away from home.

We grabbed our ropes and took off. There was two old boys working the pens on horseback and Deke asked them if we could borrow their horses so we could catch that bull.

Well, them boys give us their horses, and me and Deke lit out.

Deke closed in on him and got a loop around his horns and turned him back just as slick as you please. But when I come up to throw my heel loop, that old bull slipped down and my loop hit his side.

Before I could get my loop built again, that big devil got up and took off again. Deke was tied off hard and fast to his saddle horn, and that bull jerked Deke's horse down and dragged him twenty feet before he could get up.

Deke's horse was having a fit trying to stay away from that bull, and it was all he could do to stay in the saddle.

Well, I closed in behind him, and this time I threw a clean loop and double-hocked that joker. Me and Deke stretched them ropes real tight, and it was all them little horses could do to hold that big old Brahma bull. He was floundering around on the ground like a 1700-pound fish.

I thought sure them ropes was gonna break, but they held. We must of kept him that way for a half hour before he finally ran out of steam.

I got off of my horse and slipped Deke's loop off of his horns and around his neck so we could choke him down. And then I took my loop off of both his legs and put it around one of his legs so he could stand up. Deke got in front of him and I got behind him, and we marched him three-legged back to the railroad car and got him loaded back up without any more trouble to speak of.

Them horses was just clean worn out, and when we give them back to them old boys, Deke give them a dollar apiece and told them we appreciated it.

We was mighty glad to get out of them Kansas City stockyards, and it seemed like them bulls settled down a little bit when we did. Not much, but a little bit.

The next time we stopped to take on water, me and Deke got out to stretch our legs.

"You know, pard, I've been thinking. We got a little over four hundred dollars and another two hundred coming when we get back to El Paso. That's a whole lot of loot. Reckon we ought to put it in a bank or something?"

"I don't know, Deke. Them banks get robbed every once in a while. I'd feel like a stomp-down fool if we put all that money in a bank and it got robbed. I'd just as live for us to keep it."

"Good thinking, pard, good thinking. You know, we're gonna have about six hundred dollars. We could put us a down payment on a little spread of our own."

"Well, Deke, I'll be glad to do it if that's what you want to do. But it seems to me like a man gets tied down to a spread of his own. He don't never get the chance to go nowhere or nothing. Hell, all he's got time to do is work cows and talk about cows and worry about cows and buy cows and sell cows. I like it mighty well, Deke, with just me and you riding where we want to and doing what we damn please. It might not suit a lot of folks, but it suits me."

"Good thinking, pard, good thinking. You know I've always kinda wanted to go down to Mexico City and hang out down there for a while."

"Yeah, and Deke, I always kinda wanted to go and see the ocean. I talked to a feller one time that seen it, and he said that it stretched out so far you couldn't imagine it. He said that it was blue and that them waves just kept a-coming up on the shore. I'd purely love to see that."

"Me, too, pard, and you know what else I'd like to see?

I'd give a month's pay to see one of them elephants."

Well, the train whistle started blowing and me and Deke got back in the car, thinking about all the places we wanted to go and all the things we wanted to see.

Deke said, "Pard, what you say we deliver Mr. Ketchum's bulls and draw our pay and get our horses and light out for Mexico City?"

"Yeah, Deke, and then we could come back up through California and see the ocean and all. Hell, we got enough money to last us a month of Sundays. Let's just do us some traveling."

I was getting real excited and I think Deke was, too.

That night I dreamed about the ocean. Me and Deke was sitting up on this high hill and the ocean was stretched out down below us and there was an elephant swimming around in it. Oh, it was a dandy dream.

The next morning when we woke up, we looked out the window and could see these fellers driving a big beef herd off in the distance, and we figured we must be getting mighty close to Texas.

In two more days we pulled into El Paso, and two gladder cowboys you ain't never seen. Mr. Ketchum and Chester Penrose and a couple of hands was waiting for us, and Mr. Ketchum couldn't wait to eyeball them bulls. We got them unloaded and turned them over to his cowhands, and he was a mighty proud man.

Deke said, "Mr. Ketchum, when can we draw our pay? Me and my pardner was kinda itching to be on our way."

"Be in my office in two hours," he said, and Mr. Ketchum and Chester Penrose got back in the buckboard and drove away.

Me and Deke went into town and eat us a right sizable

meal, laid in as many supplies as we could carry, and went to the livery stable for our horses. We was saddled and packed, and we tied our horses up outside of Mr. Ketchum's office right at the time he had said.

We walked into his office just as big as you please. There won't nobody there but him and Chester Penrose.

Deke said, "Mr. Ketchum, we've come to get paid."

Mr. Ketchum cleared his throat and said, "Well, boys, I've been thinking about that, and those Brahma bulls have done a considerable bit of damage to my railroad car. It was your jobs to protect my property."

"You didn't say nothing about no railroad car when we took the job. You said that our jobs would be to protect them bulls, and you can see for yourself that they was in good health."

I piped up and said, "Besides, Mr. Ketchum, them bulls was as wild as mustangs. Me and Deke couldn't do nothing about them tearing up that railroad car short of shooting them."

"My mind is made up. I'm deducting $150 for the damage to the car, and the twenty dollars that I advanced you. So here's thirty dollars and we're even. If you don't want the thirty dollars, you can just leave. That's all I have to say on the subject."

"That won't the deal, Mr. Ketchum. You said if we brought them bulls back in good shape, you was gonna give us two hundred dollars. Anything less is cheating."

Chester Penrose had been sitting in a corner all this time and hadn't said a solitary word. Now, he stood up and said, "Are you calling Mr. Ketchum a cheat?"

"Reckon I am," Deke said, and Chester Penrose walked over to where Deke was standing.

Things was getting might tight in that room. Chester Penrose got right up in Deke's face and said, "How would you like to spend the night in a pine box, cowboy?"

Well, Deke didn't wait. He smacked old Chester Penrose right in the chops, and I jumped in at the same time and grabbed his gun hand. Deke jerked the colt out of Chester's holster before he even knew what was happening. Deke handed me the pistol and proceeded to put a whipping on Chester Penrose that he ain't likely to ever forget. Chester Penrose won't nothing without that gun. He fell apart real fast and all the fight went out of him. He looked like a limp dishrag.

Deke said, "Now, Mr. Ketchum, do you want to pay us what you owe us, or do you want my pardner to shoot you right in the belly?"

Mr. Ketchum got mighty busy counting out two hundred dollars.

Deke said, "You don't owe us but a hundred and eighty, Mr. Ketchum. Take out for the advance."

Mr. Ketchum took twenty dollars off the pile and handed the rest to Deke.

"Mr. Penrose, we didn't mean you no harm. We was just getting what was rightfully ours. Your gun will be on the desk in the outside office, but if you open that door before me and my pardner get out the front door, I'm gonna use it on you. Let's go, pard."

We backed out the door and closed it. I emptied Chester Penrose's colt and dropped it on the desk, and me and Deke went out that door like a ball of fire. We jumped on them horses and made for the border, a-spurring and a-whipping. We didn't slow down till we was about five miles inside Mexico, and then we rested the horses and took off again.

That night we had a cold camp. We was afraid to build a fire for fear somebody was on our backtrail.

The next night we didn't build a fire either. But by the third night, we figured we was safe. We had our first hot vittles in three days, and they sure tasted good.

After we eat, we was sitting around the fire drinking coffee. Deke said, "You know, pard, I sure am glad to be out of that damn railroad car and out of that damn New York City, New York."

"Me, too, Deke. It sure seems good to be out in the open again. I don't never want to take another trip like that. And then that sidewinding son of a bitch didn't want to give us our fair money. I say, to hell with him and that damn Chester Penrose, too!"

"Well, we give him his, didn't we pard?"

"We damn sure did, Deke. I don't reckon that we can ever go back to El Paso again. I'll bet you Chester Penrose and Mr. Ketchum is both as mad as a trapped grizzly."

"Ain't no loss, not going back to El Paso. Just another damn border town. When you've seen one of 'em, you've seen all of 'em. Night, pard."

"Night, Deke."

We drifted off to sleep and I expect that both of us was thinking how good it was sleeping on the ground again with a saddle for a pillow.

I woke up at sunrise feeling as fine as frog hair. I figured I'd start a fire and get the coffee going before Deke woke up. I rustled up a little wood and got the fire going and the coffee smelling good and went over to wake up Deke.

I was just about to roust him out when I seen something that almost made my heart stop. Right beside Deke's head

was a great big rattlesnake, all coiled up and ready to
do business.

I was in one hell of a mess. I knew that if I woke Deke
up and he moved, that big devil would bite him right in the
head and Deke would probably be dead in a few minutes. I
just didn't know what to do. I knew I had to do something,
and right about then I seen Deke's eyes pop open.

"Don't move, Deke. Don't move a muscle. There's a
rattler right beside your head."

"What you gonna do, pard?"

"Let me find a forked stick and I'll try to pin his head
down and grab him. Now, don't you move, Deke."

"I ain't gonna move, pard. Don't you worry about
that."

Well, I went and found me a forked stick and eased up
toward that rattlesnake. I was scared to death that he was
gonna bite Deke before I could get him pinned down.

"Well, here goes nothing," I thought, and I eased that
stick up over the rattler's head and jammed it down hard. I
got him.

I had just grabbed him up behind the head when I heard
somebody say, "Don't move."

"I ain't gonna move till you tell me to, pard. I heard you
the first time," Deke said.

"I didn't say nothing," I said. "And besides, you can
move now. I've got this rascal caught."

"Well, who said it?" Deke got up off his bedroll.

"I said don't move," and then Chester Penrose stepped
out of the brush with his colt in his hand and the hammer
back. He had two black eyes and his face was all swoll up,
but you could tell he was really enjoying having the drop
on us.

Charlie Daniels

Deke was standing between me and him, and I was still down on the ground holding that rattler with my hand behind Deke's saddle.

"Did you two saddletramps really think that you could beat up on Chester Penrose and get away with it? You poor miserable fools. I'm gonna kill you so slow it's gonna take all day to die. I'm gonna shoot your kneecaps off first," and he started to aim that colt at Deke's knee.

As soon as I seen his hand move, I flung that rattlesnake at him just as hard as I could. That rattler hit him right in the face and wrapped up all around his neck. Chester Penrose screamed like a woman and started grabbing his throat.

Now, a man can't fight rattlesnakes and shoot at the same time, and he dropped that pistol right on the ground. Quick as a wink, Deke grabbed up that gun.

"Get it off, get it off! Please get it off!"

It took me and Deke a while to figure out how to get that rattler off of Chester Penrose without getting bit. But we finally did. And old Chester passed out on the ground, cold.

When he came around, Deke had that colt pressed right up against his temples.

"I ought to blow you to smithereens, Penrose. You're a polecat son of a bitch and don't even deserve to live. What do you think we ought to do with him, pard?"

"Hell, as far as I'm concerned we can take his horse and strip him naked and leave him out here for the coyotes."

Now, Chester Penrose might not a-been afraid to face a man with a gun, but you could tell by the look in his eyes that he didn't like the prospect of being left on foot with no clothes and no water, a hundred miles from nowhere.

"I'll tell you what let's do, pard. Let's see how he feels about it. How about it, Penrose?"

"I ain't got nothing against you boys. It wasn't nothing personal. Mr. Ketchum was hopping mad and offered me five hundred dollars to track you down and do away with you. I'd a-been willing to forget about the beating."

Well, we knew he was lying. He'd a-killed both of us right then if he'd had a chance. But me and Deke hadn't never killed nobody in our whole lives, and we didn't want to start now.

"I think we'd better keep his gun, pard. Look and see if he's got another one anywhere."

I searched him and found a Derringer and took a 30/30 carbine out of his saddle boot.

We let him get on his horse and Deke said, "You ride away slow, Penrose, and if you even so much as look, back, I'm gonna put a 30/30 slug right in the back of your head. And if you ever come gunning for me or my pardner again, you won't get off so light. And you can tell Amos Ketchum that, too. Now git."

Chester Penrose mounted up mighty careful and we watched him till he rode out of sight. He never did look back.

Me and Deke broke camp and took off out of there. We never did see Chester Penrose nor Mr. Ketchum again. And I don't believe we ever will. I think they've had enough of me and Deke.